Previous books by James Malloy:

Harlem's Love

HARLEM'S LOVE 2

HARLEM'S LOVE 2

JAMES MALLOY

Good Stories

This book is a work of fiction. The names, characters and events in this book are the products of the author's imagination or are used fictitiously. Any similarity to real persons living or dead is coincidental and not intended by the author.

Harlem's Love 2

Published by Good Stories Publishing

The cover design, interior formatting, typesetting, and editorial work for this book are entirely the product of the author. Gatekeeper Press did not participate in and is not responsible for any aspect of these elements.

Cover images: eldadcarin (Woman in snowstorm at Harlem Manhattan), iStockphoto.com/Srobertcicchetti (Central Park Bridge in the snow).

Library of Congress Control Number: 2021939329

ISBN (paperback): 9781662912979

eISBN: 9781662912986

CONTENTS

Chapter One	The Rush	1
Chapter Two	Keep Calm	9
Chapter Three	The Visit	16
Chapter Four	Hearsay	21
Chapter Five	I Needed This	25
Chapter Six	I'm Ready	28
Chapter Seven	Encouragement	32
Chapter Eight	The Second Visit	35
Chapter Nine	May Growing Up	38
Chapter Ten	The Streets Made Me Cold	43
Chapter Eleven	The Foster Home	47
Chapter Twelve	Tell Me What Happened!!!!	52
Chapter Thirteen	My Friend	57
Chapter Fourteen	Back To The Hellhole	60
Chapter Fifteen	Where Is That Letter?	68

Chapter Sixteen Spanish Fly 76
Chapter Seventeen Welcome to The Family 86
Chapter Eighteen And Then This 94
Chapter Nineteen Pointless 104
Chapter Twenty Family Ties 110
Chapter Twenty-One Perfect Timing 124
Chapter Twenty-Two Why Not 135
Chapter Twenty-Three Say No!!!! 141
Chapter Twenty-Four The Next Day 149
Chapter Twenty-Five Running 161

Chapter One

THE RUSH

I remembered telling the one dude that told Auntie and I about May, "Nigga, we going to get back up. Real talk. I need to know more about this nigga Hector."

Funny-looking dude. Tried to sound sincere and shit. "No doubt, no doubt."

This dude was a nobody. You know, like a person you just bump into from time to time. Or you just see them.

The whole time Unc, Auntie, and I were walking, his voice kept playing in my head. I knew he knew more than he said, and that shit made me anxious.

Auntie yelled, "Papi, slow down!"

I looked back at her. "Auntie, I'm just trying to—"

Before I had a chance to finish, Unc interrupted, "Nephew, you moving like you about to hurt something."

Then he stopped me to get my attention.

"Listen, we trying to find out what happened to May, too, but we got to use our heads. You understand?"

On some real shit, I wasn't feeling Unc at this time, but I answered, "Yeah."

"Now, first let's try some hospitals in Brooklyn and then go from there," Unc suggested. He was right. I was tripping, so I fell back a little and paid attention.

So, we all jumped on the A train and shot to Brooklyn. Once we arrived, Auntie began to call a number of hospitals, but we had no luck. Everyone just kept telling us the same thing: "No, we don't have a Princess Malloy." However, Auntie said she did notice something about one of the hospitals—instead of saying, "No, we don't have her," they said, "We're not allowed to give that information out."

That was at Brookdale University Hospital. So we hurried and made our way over there. When we got inside, we walked over to a registration desk. There was a lady whose name tag read Almedia. She asked, "Hey, may I help you?"

We all answered, "Yes, we were hoping you had a patient here by the name of Princess Malloy."

We all stood there and watched her scroll through the names she had on her sheet. I don't know about everybody else, but I was shocked as hell when she answered, "Yes, we do. She's in room 3031."

We just looked at each other. The receptionist was like, "Yaw okay?"

We all answered at the same time, "Yeah, yeah, we good."

She pointed us in the direction of the elevator that would take us up to 3031. We got on the elevator and caught it up to the fifth floor. We were all silent. Nobody said a word.

This whole thing felt strange. My heart was pounding, and honestly, I didn't know what to say.

The elevator doors opened, and we made our way to 3031. When we got to the door of May's room, she was lying there with tubes and IVs attached to her. A white sheet covered her from the chest down. Unc and I stood there, damn near in the doorway. Auntie instantly began crying. Wiping her tears away, she made her way over to May.

Sobbing, she asked, "May, baby, can you hear me?"

May just laid there motionless, with her eyes closed.

"May, baby, if you can hear me, I'm here. It's your auntie."

I felt terrible. The only thing that kept running through my mind was who did this. But I had to go over and say something. So, I made my way over and stood next to her. Her face and lips looked a little swollen, and her hair was all over her head. It was her; she didn't look the same, but at the same time, she didn't look badly injured.

I grabbed her hand to say something, but right when I was about to speak, I was interrupted by her doctor, who was now coming through the door. His accent sounded Filipino.

"Hi, everyone. I'm Dr. Erango. Are you guys family members?"

Auntie spoke, "Yes, we are really close friends."

The doc stood five-eleven, fairly brown skin, and straight black hair that was shaped in a bob cut. He stood directly across from us and addressed us about May's condition.

"Well, her condition is stabilizing, but a little slower than usual."

Unc surprised me when he spoke.

"Hold up, Doc. We don't even know what happened to her."

"She was brought into the ER with a gunshot wound to the chest. The X-rays that were taken showed a bullet lodged against her second rib on an upward path to the heart. I determined it was safer to leave the bullet embedded deep in her chest rather than to operate. It would decrease the chance of death, especially of the baby."

My heart stopped, and the room got completely quiet. Well, at least that is what I thought. It was like I zoned out, but when I came back, Auntie was in a rage.

"Doc, are you fucking serious?"

"Yes, ma'am, I am."

"Well, how many months?"

"Six to eight weeks."

Auntie yelled, "Oh my God, I can't believe this shit! Is the baby okay?"

"Yes, the baby is fine."

"Papi. Do you hear this shit? Do you?"

Not saying the baby wasn't cool, but this whole thing was a fucking nightmare, and I had to wake up. I was now sitting down, and Unc was standing over me with his hand on my shoulder.

Auntie was still in disbelief. "What the fuck?"

Unc yelled, "Calm down, Wilma! Can't you see he's going through it?"

"Can't I see? I'll tell you what I see. I see a woman laid upon a bed, half dead, pregnant with Papi's baby. That's what I see."

Unc didn't respond to her. Instead, he said, "Mike, I'm going to walk your auntie out into the hall so she can get herself together. You be strong, nephew. It is what it is. You got yourself into this mess."

As soon as they left, the doc said quietly, "Sir, I'm going to need some info on her."

I just looked at him.

Now standing directly in front of me, he continued, "I need to know her insurance information or if she has any at all."

I stood up, walked maybe a few steps away from him, scratched the back of my head, and said, "Doc, honestly, I don't know a lot about her." Knowing I didn't know any of her friends or family members, I lied, "But I can find out."

He replied, "Thanks. That would be great. Now I'm going to leave you guys alone."

"All right, Doc. Thanks, man."

As he was walking past me, I stopped him. "Hey, how long will it take before she starts talking again?"

"Well, like I said before, she's recovering well, but slowly. As far as her being responsive, she is in and out due to the high dosage of medication. The nurses had her responding a little earlier today."

"Oh, okay, Doc. Thanks again."

When he left, I walked over to her. I just stood there and stared at her. Then I grabbed her hand. It was like all of a sudden I became angry. Still holding her hand, but now a little tighter, I whispered loudly, "May, what the fuck were you thinking? After everything we talked about. I told you that clown-ass nigga wasn't no good."

It was like she was awake, and I was talking to her.

I continued, "Now, look. You all fucked up, and you know I'm not going to let this slide. You don't worry about shit, May. I got his ass. Real talk."

Right when I was finished talking, I felt her hand grip mine tighter. Then she moved her head from side to side. I think she was telling me no.

"May, chill. Relax. I got this, okay? You get better. I'll be back."

It sounded painful, but she moaned something out. At this time, Auntie and Unc were walking back in. They caught me teary-eyed. Auntie ran straight over and gave me a hug. Then she leaned away from me, looked me in the face, and said, "Papi, it's going to be all right."

Slightly pushing her away, I said, "I know, Auntie, I know."

As I walked off, she tried to hold my hand, but I pulled away and walked out. Then she tried to follow me, but Unc interrupted, "Wilma, let him go. I got him."

"I know, Shaheed, but I never seen Papi act like this. I don't like the way he looks. It's not like him. He's about to do something dumb."

"Okay, let me go talk to him."

"Please, please do."

I started walking down the hall. I heard Unc yell, "Hey, neph."

I kept walking.

"Yo, neph! Stop right there. I need to talk to you."

One thing I did do was show Unc respect, and no matter how upset I was, I wasn't about to disrespect him now.

So I stopped and leaned against the wall.

"So, you about to walk straight out there, let everybody know your business, then make your move?"

"Unc, you don't understand. That's crazy how they did her. She's good people."

"I do understand. You trying to find the nigga that did this and make things right. I feel you, but I don't like the way you moving. First of all, when you are about to make a big move, you never do it out of anger. That can cause you to make a clumsy move. Second, never tell a soul. Niggas are not as real as you think they are. Only you can tell on yourself."

Then he grabbed me real tight and whispered in my ear, "Nephew, I know you about to kill this dude, but be smart about it."

I gripped Unc tight as well. "I will, Unc, I will."

I kinda gave Unc a look like, "What you know about that life?" but then I thought about the stories Auntie told me. She said Unc was a monster in his prime. A true gangster, he ran with Nicki and Guy during the times they were getting busy. Very loyal, but cold-blooded, and responsible for a lot of unsolved shit. It wasn't until he got caught up with racketeering, kidnapping, and drug-related charges that he changed.

After doing fifteen straight years in upstate New York, Unc came home and found his true love, Auntie. And another reason he stayed focused was because Auntie stayed on his ass. Unc did some real-live shit.

I looked at Unc with a smile. "I feel you, Old G. I won't let us down."

At the time, I didn't see Auntie. She was still in the room with May. So, I figured I'd make a move and slide away from the hospital.

"Unc, Ima shoot to the crib and get some rest. Tell Auntie I'll catch up with her there and May, if she can hear you, that I'll be back later."

Unc gave me this look like "Are you sure you're, okay?" and said, "Okay, neph. Be easy."

Chapter Two

KEEP CALM

It was around two thirty when I hit the block, so there weren't a lot of people out. I did run into a few niggas wanting some green. With all this shit going on with May, my mind wasn't completely clear, but I had to get back on my grind. On some real shit, all that kept running through my mind was Hector, but I had to keep calm.

Right when I hit my steps to go into my building, I thought, *Shit, let me go holler at Willie real quick.* Plus I had to break down those ten pounds of green that Steve threw me.

I had never mentioned this before, but there had been times I went to Willie's place and noticed a short little lady walking away from his house. The crazy thing is I never saw her face. She would always be walking in the same direction as me. She was a short, skinny lady. Always seemed to have the same clothes on, or I probably wasn't paying a lot of attention to her. But her black hat and her blue jean outfit that looked completely worn out was all that I remembered, and that's what she had on today.

When I went to open the door, it was stopped by the top lock chain.

I was like, "Yo, Willie."

He ran to the door. "Oh shit, Mike, hold on."

He left the chain on the door and ran off. I was thinking, *What the hell?*

After two minutes of disappearing, he came back. Taking the chain off the door, he whispered, "My fault. Baby, come in."

"Damn, you all right?"

"Yeah, I'm good. Why you ask that?"

"Nigga, don't play dumb. I saw your shorty just leave."

"Man, you lost your motherfucking mind if you think I'm fucking that."

"Hold up, Willie. Who said anything about fucking?"

He got all serious.

"Look, man, I told you. She's like my people."

Now, we all know that when a person reacts too dramatically and keeps repeating himself, then he's telling a lie, and that's how he was acting.

"Yeah, nigga, I hear you."

Then I thought, *Damn, nigga, keep it real. I'm not dumb. If it's that bad, then stop fucking her.*

Then he changed the subject up. "Yo, I'm sorry to hear about May."

"Yeah, man, that's some crazy shit."

Taking a seat at his kitchen table, he looked up at me. "So when is the funeral?"

"Funeral? Man, she's not dead. I just left her at the hospital."

"Nah, you serious?"

"Yeah, man, I'm dead serious."

"Damn, niggas running around here got her dead."

"Nah, she good, but she's in bad shape. She was shot once in the chest."

"Shit. Did they say who done it?"

"They keep saying this Hector dude."

"Shit, well you already know. Just be safe."

"For sure."

I felt a little relief. The last few days before I saw May, I was down. I'm not saying I was all the way back, but I could just think a lot clearer now. Also, this baby situation had me fucked up. But, overall, it was time to get this bread.

When Steve had hit me with the work, I had stashed it in my safe at Willie's.

Walking in the direction of my trap room, I said, "Yo, Willie, Ima shoot in here and bag my work up. I got you when I'm done."

"All right, Mike, you good."

Walking into my trap room, it was like I saw flashes of May. The shit I had been through with her and this room would stain anyone's memory. Anyway, I turned the TV on and walked over to my safe to grab my work. I took out a pound of weed and locked the nine back up. I grabbed my baggies and scale from under the bathroom sink then started bagging my work up.

Altogether I bagged up thirteen ounces, and the other three I broke down to nics and dimes. I was determined to get back after the big hit I had taken from my cousin robbing me. I locked the thirteen ounces away in the safe, and the other three ounces of nics and dimes, I stashed in my couch area. I was ready to get back. My money was low and didn't feel comfortable.

When I walked out of my trap room, Willie was sitting at the table as usual. I had forgotten to leave out some green for him, but before I had a chance to make those arrangements for him, he said, "I'm good on the green, but I was hoping you could give me some money instead."

I knew what time it was. Willie was after some hard, aka crack. I was beginning to be a little concerned for this dude. Lately, that had been his drug of choice.

I thought to myself, *Shit, I'm trying to make some bread, not give it away,* but on some real shit, I was using his spot.

"Here, Willie, this all I got."

I gave him forty dollars.

He was like, "Good look, Mike."

I didn't say much more. I just walked out.

He called me right when I reached the sidewalk.

With a serious look on his face, he said, "Yo, Mike, you be careful out there, you hear me?"

"No doubt, bro. I'll probably be back later."

My plan was to post up on the block for a while. Money was coming slow at first, but then it picked up. In the process of doing everything, I bumped into Crazy and Loc. They asked me about the May situation, so I gave them the rundown. They didn't say too much; they just noticed right away I didn't look comfortable. One thing about my niggas was when one hurt, we all hurt.

Loc dapped me up. "So when we going to handle this dude?"

Crazy interrupted, "Who the fuck is the dude, and where the fuck he be?"

They just kept going on and on. I cut them off, "Yo, I barely know shit about this clown myself. All I know is Hector is from the Bronx."

They were like, "Okay, we going to keep our ears to the streets."

I smiled at my people. "No doubt, no doubt."

Then we started talking about some other shit. In the midst of all this, the work was moving. Before you knew it, it was time to re-up, but shit, I was getting hungry. So I told them I was out, then shot up to the crib.

When I got upstairs, Unc was in the living room, and Auntie was coming from the kitchen. She had a glass of water in one hand and pills in the other.

"Auntie, you okay?"

"Yeah, I'm okay. I just need to lie down for a few."

I hugged her, but she barely hugged me back. She was mad at me.

I felt terrible. Auntie had never asked for any of this, and now I had her stressing.

Still hugging her, I said, "Auntie, I'm sorry for all this, and I'm going to make things better. I'm not going to do anything dumb."

Almost in a crying voice, she replied, "Promise me, Papi."

She caught me off guard, and I hated lying to her.

She spoke again, "Promise me, Papi."

I thought, *Damn, this is crazy.*

Then I said it, "I promise."

Then she gave me a tight hug that seemed like it lasted forever. The whole time she was hugging me, I was thinking to myself, *Sorry, Auntie, sorry.* Not because of the drama I caused, but because I knew I couldn't keep my promise.

"Okay, Papi, I'm about to lie down. The food is on the stove."

Honestly, I didn't feel like eating, but I grabbed my plate and went into the kitchen, where Unc was. Unc and Auntie must have had a long talk about me, and I could tell that it wasn't a good one. He still bussed it up with me though. We had a long, serious talk. Truly, it was some shit I needed to hear. He told me to go back over to the hospital to talk to May.

I quickly interrupted, "Hold on, Unc. I thought the doc said she was out of it."

"No, he said she was in and out of it. She talked to us a little while after you left."

I thought right away, *I got to get over there ASAP*, but then I thought, *Maybe I should just grind the night out and then shoot over there tomorrow morning.* It was getting late.

I told Unc that I would get back up with him and shot downstairs. There were a lot more people out, and it seemed like the word had spread quickly about May. Niggas were dapping me up like crazy. I felt the love for sure. They kept asking me questions about Hector. I told them, "On some real shit, I don't know, but if ya find out, let me know."

While all the talking was taking place, niggas were copping green, so shit was good. I grind for a few more hours, then took it down for the night.

Chapter Three

THE VISIT

When I walked into May's room, I was surprised. The scenery was completely different. She was sitting up in the bed, eating. As soon as she saw me, her face lit up with a big smile. I thought right away, *Damn, I never saw her smile like that before. She must really miss me.* I know that sounds a little strange, but she wasn't the cheesy-smiling type. The most I had ever seen was a slick grin.

I stopped right where I was standing. "Oh, you miss me?"

She changed her smile slightly. "No, nigga. Where you been?"

"What?"

I walked over and gave her a hug, but she was unable to hug me back because of the pain from the gunshot wound to the chest.

So I pushed her arm down and said, "Well, I miss your punk ass."

With her raspy voice and still sounding in pain, she didn't waste no time getting nasty. First, she complained about the doc and nurses that kept fucking with her, then she yelled, "Nigga, what the fuck?"

I responded, "What?"

"Don't what me. You put something in me, dumbass. I don't like this dumbass feeling, and what am I supposed to do with it?"

"Damn, May, chill. We got to get you right first."

"Chill, my ass."

"Be quiet before I take your food."

"You can have this nasty-ass shit. I go back to the streets."

"Oh, no, you won't, nasty ass."

"This food is nasty."

"Yo, you got nerve calling something nasty."

"Yo, you really got me twisted, nigga. I never ate shit from trash cans. I stole my shit from stores."

Then she lay back like she was out of breath. "Man, they said that they going to keep me for another two weeks because of this thing."

"What thing?"

"The thing you put in me."

"Yo, it's not a thing."

May was coming back to her normal self, but she still had a ways to go. She was definitely happy to see me. She just kept going from one conversation to another. What was funny was the whole time, she was out of breath.

I started laughing. "Yo, what kind of meds they got your ass on? I never heard you talk so much, May."

She laughed, "Fuck you, son."

It was getting late, and on some real shit, I was thinking about crashing here. In the room was a small reclining sofa.

"Yo, May, ring the nurses. I need a pillow."

"What?"

"You heard me. Shit, I'm about to crash out. I'm tired."

She didn't reply; she just rang the bell.

The nurse came in. "Hey, you okay?"

May, dumbass, said, "I don't need you. He do."

I just looked at her. Then I asked the nurse if they had an extra pillow or two.

"Yes, I'll be right back," Then she paused. "Oh, you need a blanket too."

"Yes, thanks."

Then I thought, *Shit, I'm good now.* After I got myself nice and comfortable, I lay back with my toes facing the ceiling and my fingers crossed behind my head. About five minutes into relaxing, May started talking again.

"Mike, my father told me that I was born in this same hospital."

I lifted my head up in disbelief. She never spoke about her family. But I didn't interrupt. I just laid my head back down.

She continued, "He told me, 'May, I remember the very night you were born. I was rushing over to the hospital. It was raining and thundering its ass off. When I reached the room, your mother was giving the nurses hell. I was really concerned because your mother was strung out on drugs and didn't look well lying there. She was really small and had dark marks all over her body.'

'Your mother yelled, 'Get this damn baby outta me. I'm in fucking pain, assholes!'

'The nurse said, 'Ma'am, you have to relax.'

'Nah, fuck that. Take it out and give it to his bitch ass.'

'She was talking about me. I just stood there, looking out the window, listening to her throw a fit. Maybe a half hour after that, you came. You came straight out, screaming at the top of your lungs.

'The nurses set you on your mother's chest. She looked at you, then looked at me and said, 'I guess she looks like you.' She smiled at you, then gave you a kiss. Then she told the nurse to give you to me because she had somewhere to be.

'The nurse put you in my hands and almost immediately, you stopped crying. Then she asked, 'What should we name her?'

'I looked at you without a thought and said, 'Princess. Princess Malloy.' Your mother looked over with a slight frown.

'Let me tell you, May—your mother was a good person. I mean, she had a big heart, but the drugs destroyed her. I know for a fact that deep down inside, she was crying for you.

'When I first met your mother, it was 1966 at a book festival in Brooklyn. She was standing in line buying a book. After an hour of smooth talking her, she finally let me give her my number. Let's just say she was beautiful, and I couldn't resist. It took months before we started dating. She didn't play hard to get; she *was* hard to get. She was short. Long, pretty black hair, and her skin tone was amazing. Just like you.

'Your mother was an elementary school teacher. A very loving and caring person. Sometimes I blame myself for your mother's change of life. My boys and I would drink occasionally, but I took it to another level. I started drinking alcohol a lot and became an alcoholic. That pushed her away from me. So far away that she left me for another man.

'I don't know what happened after that, but she came back, stealing from me and even bringing men into my home when I wasn't there. Shortly after that, I found out that she was using drugs. Everything went downhill from there. She was watching you one day when some maniac she had stolen money from broke into our home and killed her in front of you.'

"Yo, nigga, you asleep?" May asked. "Never mind, stay asleep."

"Nah, nah, I'm good. That's some crazy shit. So, who would watch you?"

"My father said that my aunt Mickey would watch me when he would have to work. But get some rest. I'll talk to you another time about it."

No bullshit. I was into her story, but I was also sleepy as shit.

"Alright, I'll talk to you tomorrow."

Chapter Four

HEARSAY

The next morning came fast. When I looked around, I noticed May wasn't in her bed. After I got myself together, I walked to the nurses' station to ask about May. The nurse told me that she had gone for some tests and that she should be back soon.

On my way out of the hospital, Auntie was walking in.

"Hey, Papi, I was wondering where you were."

"Hey, Auntie, I crashed over here last night."

"Oh. How's May?"

"She's good. They just took her to have some tests done. But she should be back soon."

"Okay. I'm not doing anything; I'll just go up anyway."

"All right. I'm going to the crib to get dressed."

She gave me a hug and said that Unc had an emergency and that he would be gone for a week. I told her cool and that I'd get with her later.

I got about two blocks away from the crib, and you wouldn't believe who I bumped into. The nigga that told me about what happened to May. I was starting to think, *What, is this nigga watching me?* I thought immediately, *Shit, I need to know more about this clown, Hector.*

I had to get on this dude's good side, so I walked up to him with a smile. "What up, son? Glad I ran into you again."

I didn't even know this dude's name.

He was like, "Yeah, it's all good. What's up?"

"Not much. Just coming from seeing May."

"Who?"

"You remember. The girl Hector shot."

"Oh shit. She's good?"

"Yeah, she's straight."

"Yeah, like I was saying, I didn't know if she was dead or alive. That was the word."

"I remember you saying that, but I was hoping you could tell me a little more about the word."

We posted up in front of the African joint on 125th. And then he started giving me the rundown.

"Look, son. First off, Hector is a snake. A real bad person. I used to fuck with Hector real tough when I was younger until I caught a charge behind him.

"One day he asked me to walk with him to his cousin's house. When we got there, he said his cousin acted funny when he brought people to his crib, so he asked me to wait out front. So, I was like, 'All right, cool.'

"He left and came back in twenty minutes. He told me that his cousin wasn't there, but he was on his way. He gave me his description and told me if I saw him, to tell him that I'd be right back. So, I was like, 'Where the fuck you going?'

"Nigga told me that he had to shoot to the corner store real quick and that he didn't want to miss him. I was like, 'Hurry the fuck up, son.' Let's just say his cousin didn't pop up, but the Jakes did.

"Yo, that was never his cousin's spot. He went into some old man's house, tied him up, beat him, and robbed him. And since I was just standing out front, I became the immediate suspect. When they took me to the precinct, the old man identified me as the robber. I did five years behind some bullshit I didn't do. That nigga is a piece of shit."

"Damn, that's crazy as fuck, but I need to know about May, the girl he shot. How you know about that?"

"There's this dude named Junie. Hector's right hand. Now, June fucked with me because we done some real shit together, but not to the point where he would tell me some deep shit about Hector. So, Eric, my boy, he knows June well. June told Eric, and Eric told me about the drop. He said that they were laughing about it in the hood. Something about a lot of fake money and a girl getting shot."

He gave me this serious look. "Look, man, if you see Hector talking to someone, it's because either he's trying to get something from him, or he's trying to use him to get something. He lives in the Bronx, East Tremont."

Shit. I started thinking, *I heard Steve talk about East Tremont. I got to talk to Steve about this shit, but he's always busy. He told me it's crazy wild over there.*

He continued, "Yo, this nigga get high, but he be having mad bread too. You can't really tell because the nigga stay fly. Shit, he be having more bread than the niggas that be on the block every day. And the reason for that is because he lives inside an abandoned building with the fens. They said he be beating the fens, bossing them around, making them spend their money with him. Then, during the day, he hangs out with the rest of the niggas, trying to blend in, but he sticks out like a sore thumb. His skin tone always looks dull, and his lips always look dry. Sometimes he even goes without a cut for a while.

"I don't know, son, but that nigga is a piece of shit for real."

I looked at him. "Yo, good look. I appreciate it."

I was far from slow, and this nigga could be telling me anything. What I did know was if he was on some slick shit, he was going to catch one too. For one, it seemed like this dude was going a little overboard with helping me. I just didn't know. I couldn't have this dude being two-sided, so I hit him with the fadeaway.

"Yo, like I said, thanks for the info, but I don't know her like that to be getting into any gangster shit behind her. I thought it was someone else on some real shit."

He kinda gave me this funny look and said, "No problem."

Chapter Five

I Needed This

I told that nigga I was out and made my way to the crib. I had to take a shower and get shit situated. I had a lot of thoughts racing through my head. There was a lot of stuff going on, and it seemed like it was all at once. This year had been mad crazy. It seemed like my whole life was changing right in front of me. A child, a broad I barely knew, unintended beef, and feeling broke.

After I got dressed, I sat in the living room. Nothing on, just peace and quiet. I sat there for a few and pondered on a few things. Moving was one of the things I was considering, but I thought about Auntie being alone. I thought that I needed to talk to Unc about possibly finding a local job, so he could be home every night. As much as I loved Auntie, I couldn't let her life stop mine. Now, while I was thinking all this, my phone rang. I looked, and it was my sister calling.

I answered, "Hey, sis, what's up?"

"Hey, Mike, how you been? And what you been up to?"

"I'm good, and you?"

"We are doing fine. I'm calling you because you never think to call me."

"It's not like that, sis. I'm always thinking about you. I always think to call, but it seems like dumb shit distracts me. How's your fiancé? And when is the baby due?" Then it accidentally slipped out, "Oh shit, speaking of baby—"

But she cut me off.

"Well, the baby, which is a he, is due in three months. Now, what was you about to say?"

I paused, then laughed a little. "Shit, I still can't believe this, but I just found out that May is pregnant."

I thought that might be a bit much for Sis because she knew very little about May and the stuff that had been going on with her, but she was good with it.

"Oh, Mike, I'm so happy for ya." She went on and on, and then things went left. "So, are you working now? Does she have a job? Are you going back to school?"

She came at me hard. So, I gave her a little relief and told her that I was thinking of moving down there with her.

That changed the subject up ASAP. She was all for it. But on some real shit, I was thinking about relocating.

Sis was like, "Well, that's good. You can stay here for a while until you find a spot."

"I know, sis; I'll let you know when."

"Also, Mike. You know Mom owned the spot we used to live in. So, you can always move there. And plus, I got your check that she left you."

"What check?"

"Her life insurance check. She left us some money."

I got quiet. Shit, I was missing Mom like crazy, and just talking about her was a little too much for me at the time.

"Mike, you there?"

I had to be strong. Shit, I couldn't be weak. It was just my sister and me now. She needed to know that I was her number one supporter.

"Yeah, sis, I'm here."

"Mike she left us some money behind. I mean it's something."

"Damn, we straight, sis?"

"Yes, Mike, we good."

"Well, hold mine for me, sis. Until I come down."

"Okay. It will be in the bank."

Then there was a little pause on the phone, then she said, "Mike, I really miss Mom. Life is so different without her. And now I'm worried about Aunt Rebecca, living by herself."

"I know, sis, I miss her too. And we got to get together and go check on Aunt Rebecca. And maybe we can talk her into moving too."

"That sounds good, Mike. I hope that happens."

"It will. And while we are visiting her, we can put some flowers on Mom's grave."

"Okay, Mike. We're going to make some dates and stick to them."

We bussed it up for a while longer and then said our byes.

Chapter Six

I'M READY

I relaxed about a half hour longer, then I thought, *Shit, I got to make something happen.* So, I shot downstairs. There were a few people out. I bumped into a few cats wanting some green. Right when I was about to post up on my steps and chill, Thug Main and his cousin, Hill Top, came walking around the corner. I knew Hill Top from back in the day. He used to come and chill with us until he caught a long stretch. Some strong-armed robbery shit. When he came home, he started fucking with some broad from Rhode Island and moved over there. The nigga's street credit was good, and he was nice with his hands, so niggas didn't play with him too much. He put so much work in that niggas had named him after a violent block from his hometown. Hill Top.

"What up, Mike?" Maine asked while dapping me up.

I replied, "Shit, son, you know. Trying to maintain."

At this time, I was dapping Hill Top up.

He was like, "What's up, nigga?"

I smiled at him. "Long time no see. Nigga, I'm good."

"You sure, nigga? I'm hearing some crazy shit."

I was thinking, *Damn, news spread fast. I wonder how much Maine told him. I mean, I'm cool with Hill Top, but I'm trying to take Hector out quietly.*

"Yeah, son, shit's crazy."

"Well, nigga, Hill Top here."

Letting my hand go, he looked at me. "Yo, nigga, I'm fucking serious."

"I know, son. I'll let you know. I'm just trying to keep shit quiet, so things can take place."

I bussed it up with them for a little while longer, then Steve called.

"What up, son?"

"Shit. What's up with you?"

"Not much. Fam trying get my change back up, so I'm hugging the block, you feel me?"

"Absolutely. Well, you know I'm here for you. Just let me know when you are ready."

"No doubt. Yo, how's Grandma doing?"

"She's good, bro. Same shit though. Losing her memory."

"That's my baby. I got to go check her out. And yo, I really need to let you know what's going on with me. I'm about to make a move, son."

He laughed. "What, nigga? You good?"

"Yeah, I'm straight, but I need to talk to you. I'll tell you whenever I see your busy ass."

We both laughed for a few, then I hung up with him. Everything was going well. I mean, money was flowing continuously. About three hours later, it was time to re-up again. Plus, I had to put my bread up. So, I shot down to Willie's. When I got there, he was standing in the doorway, talking to some old head he knew. I breezed by both of them and told Willie that I was going to the back.

Once I got in the room, I opened my safe, grabbed four ounces to break down, and stashed my money away. In the process of doing that, I thought, *Damn. If I had just kept my money down here, I would have been straight. Willie is a thorough old head. He doesn't fuck with anything of mine. And he damn sure doesn't let anyone get close to it.*

Anyway, I bagged the four ounces up in nics and dimes as always. It was time to get this bread, and I was excited about it.

When I walked out of the room, Willie was still talking to his old head. But when I tried to walk around them, he stopped me and said he had something to talk to me about. So, he told his boy that he was going to get back with him. I walked over and stood by the kitchen table.

He walked over to me. "Yo, I see they finally caught up with slick-ass Eagle."

"No! What the fuck happened?"

"They said that he broke into some drug dealer's house to rob it. And while he was in there, stashing all the drugs and money in his pockets, the goddamn cops raided the crib. Let's just say that nigga had bad luck that day. And they gave him mad coke charges because he was in possession of the drugs.

On top of that, when he goes to jail, the nigga he tried to rob is going to catch up with him."

"Damn, the Eagle done fucked up bad." Then I said, "Damn. Well, that nigga had to know that his crazy-ass ways were going to catch up with him eventually. But he probably didn't expect it to be like that."

We chopped it up for a little, then I made my way back to the block, but of course, after I took care of Willie. It was getting late, so more people were out. On my way down the block, I saw Loc, Den Den, and Mitchell. I dapped them all up then asked them what they were about to get into.

Mitchell was like, "These dice nigga, Celo. What, you trying to get down?"

I laughed. "Hell, no, son. Shit, I'm trying to get my bread back up."

Loc said, "Stop playing, nigga. You got bread."

Tom, trying to manipulate a nigga, said, "Come on, Mike. You can get your money back faster like this."

I laughed again.

Maine giggled, "Shit, Mike said fuck that."

Yo, these niggas were crazy. They be talking about any and every little thing. They said that Boot, Shark, and L-Boogie were coming to get down with them too. I just posted up with them and sold some green.

I wanted to ask them what was up with Crazy, but I noticed Auntie coming around the corner.

Chapter Seven

ENCOURAGEMENT

I ran over to get her attention. "Hey, Auntie."

She stopped at the top step. Then she walked down to give me a hug and ask what I was doing.

"Nothing, Auntie. I'm just hanging out with my people."

"Are you busy right now, Papi?"

On some real shit, I already knew what tip Auntie was on. She was about to peel me about this whole thing with May.

So, I said, "Auntie, really, I'm waiting on somebody. But why? What's up?"

She just looked at me for a second. "Papi, let's go. They can wait."

I didn't say nothing. I just followed her to the elevator. The whole elevator ride was quiet, and from the expression on her face, she looked like she was about to cry.

When we got in the apartment, she walked into the living room then sat down on the couch. Then she whispered, "Papi, I failed you."

She hit me with that one.

"Hey, Auntie, why do you say that?"

"I did, Papi. I did so good with my two boys. Trying to keep you around, I let you get away with too much. I should have been a lot stricter on you about things."

She went on and on.

I interrupted, "Auntie, please stop blaming yourself for my decisions. You and Unc did stay in my shit, you know that. I'm the one who made poor decisions."

I went and sat by her. "Auntie, it's nobody's fault. Everything is going to be fine."

"I know, Papi, but May, and now, a baby."

"Hey, look, Auntie, I'm about to get shit together. I see that this shit is getting real."

I had to make her smile and brighten her back up, so I said, "Shit, if worst comes to worst, we'll just give you the baby."

She looked up instantly with a serious face. "Yeah, I hear you." Then she said, "Nah, Papi, that's your responsibility. The only way I'm doing that shit is if I absolutely have to."

Then I thought, *Shit, that might be right up Auntie's alley.* As a matter of fact, Auntie had probably already made plans for the baby. I bet you.

Anyway, she just had a long talk with me about getting a job and doing the right thing. She definitely didn't like the fact that I was out there selling weed. I sat and listened to everything she had to say. Shortly after that, the phone rang. It was Unc. I told her to tell him I said hi and that I was leaving.

She said okay, and right when I was about to close the door, she yelled, "Oh, Papi, May said to come by!"

I yelled, "Okay, Auntie, love you!"

"Love you too. And you be safe out there."

Chapter Eight

THE SECOND VISIT

The block was still jumping, so I made some more bread. Then I shot down to Willie's to lock everything away. It was now getting late, and I wanted to go check on May, so I made my way over there. When I walked into the room, she was sitting on the bed, looking through some papers.

"Hey, May, what's up with you?"

Her punk ass acted like she wasn't happy to see me.

She looked up, then back down. "Yo."

"Yo, what's up with you? Sounding all rough and rugged like a nigga."

"What? What you want me to do, jump off the bed and into your arms? Don't you see me reading?"

"Reading. Shit, I didn't think you knew how to."

"Yo, you talk, dumb as fuck."

I was like, "Yeah, whatever. What you reading anyway?"

"Some crazy shit about following up with all these different doctors. I'm telling you right now, I'm not doing none of this shit."

"Oh yes, you are."

"Okay. Watch me."

"Yo, look. I'm tired as shit. I'm going to crash over here again."

"I don't care. The blankets and shit are still over on the chair."

"Yo, May, did you really have to use the word *shit*? What, you can't talk without cussing?"

"Yo, nigga, I do and say whatever the fuck I want. I'm grown."

I didn't even respond. I walked over to her and gave her a hug that she refused to take. So, I snatched the papers out of her hand in the process. The papers looked like discharge forms.

"May, what? They about to discharge you?"

"Not today, but the doc said something about tomorrow or the following morning." Then she asked, "So, what you been up to?"

"Nothing, really. Just been trying to get my bread back up. Steve put me back on, so I been trying to move it."

"That's what's up?" Then she got real on me. "Yo, Mike, this whole shit is crazy, man. This baby, keeping these appointments, finding somewhere to live; this shit is way too much for me. I don't know what to do."

I cut her off, "Look. Peep this. Let me handle that. I got all that shit taken care of. That's the last thing you should be worried about. Just focus on getting this money, and everything else will fall into place."

"Your auntie is a very nice person. She also told me not to worry. But I do because all this shit seems weird as fuck."

At this time, the nurse came in to check May's vitals. So, I walked over to the little love seat that I had previously slept on the night before and got it ready. You know, pillows, blanket, stuff like that. I overheard the nurse saying May's blood pressure was high. So, I interrupted because May was just sitting there, saying nothing.

"Hey, excuse me, but I heard you say something about her blood pressure being too high?"

The nurse answered, "Yes, her blood pressure has been spiking a lot. Right now, it's 165/95. It's understandable because she's still in a little pain, but we want to make sure we get that stabilized before we release her. Especially with her being pregnant. Besides that, she and the baby are doing just fine. So, she should be going home in the next two days."

May, with her smart-ass mouth, said, "Yeah, you keep saying the same shit every day. I keep telling you, I'm about to walk out, bitch."

The nurse didn't respond to her silly ass. She just said that she would be right back and walked out.

After that I just sat back on the couch, kicked my boots off, and fell back. May was watching something on TV that was making me fall fast asleep. But right when I was about to go under, she woke me up.

Chapter Nine

MAY GROWING UP

"Hey, Mike."

Yooo.

"Like I was saying about when I was younger."

I looked up. Like what the hell?

I really didn't know what she was talking about, but I covered up and said, "Yeah."

"My father was a really good parent. But he had a drinking problem. He drank so much that he began getting sick from it. He would get up every morning to go to work; I mean, he'd never miss a day. But when he came home, he had to have a drink. He was all I had. People thought that we were strange because we stayed to ourselves.

"He didn't have much family. Just a sister and brother. Both of my grandparents were deceased. His brother, Jodie, lived in Philly and his sister, Mickey, lived not far from us in Brownsville, Brooklyn. My aunt Mickey was rough and rugged. Short, brown skin, and a little stocky. She fucked niggas and bitches. She had like eight kids. Four lived with her, and the rest lived with their father. Let's just say the two-year-old felt like a child of mine. But we'll get to that part in a few.

"Anyway, my aunt was the party type. Always planning some sort of party event or somehow involving herself in someone else's beef. Off the hook, she was. She would fight with a quickness.

"Back to my father. I knew things were getting really bad with him when he started missing work and going to the doctor a lot. I did everything that I could possibly do to take care of him, but I was young and still had to be at school. And when I would purposely miss school to take care of him, he would get mad and make me go.

"Every morning I put something together for us for breakfast, gave him a kiss, and then went off to school. Then one morning I went into the room and gave him a kiss, and his face felt cold. And when I tried to move him, he was stiff. I stood there, motionless. Then I lay on him and cried and cried."

I moved the blankets from my head. "Damn, May, that's crazy."

"Yeah, I know. Then I had to move to the hellhole. My aunt Mickey's place. My whole life changed dramatically from that day on. You were pretty much on your own, living with her. She told me, 'Look, you are staying here now. I don't have time for no soft shit. If you get hungry, fix yourself something to eat. If there's nothing in there, try to put something together or let me know.' I didn't know what she meant by 'put something together,' but I found out later.

"Then she gave me this serious look. 'I don't got time for the dumb shit. You hear me?'

"I answered, 'Yes, ma'am.'

"My father taught me to love and respect my elders, so that's what I did. But for some reason, I think she thought I was being a little extra. She gave me this look, like, 'This is not going to work.'

"The two-year-old baby girl, Tanesha, seemed like my child because I watched her so much. She would keep me out of school when she had something to do. I grew up loving school. I was always at the top of my class. I was a pretty smart girl, but that shit changed. I found myself failing because I missed so much time from school. It wasn't just that, though. I was also embarrassed to go to school because I wore the same dirty-ass clothes, and my hair always looked crazy. Things like soap, laundry detergent, hair grease, lotion, toothpaste, different clothes, etc., weren't a factor around there. It was rough as fuck. I was just a babysitter.

"Now, on top of all the bullshit, what really made me uncomfortable was this guy she knew that would come over and stay from time to time. He would always look at me all crazy and shit. Whenever my aunt wasn't around, he would always ask if I was hungry. And, of course, I was. Shit, there was never nothing in the refrigerator to eat. So, he would bring me cakes and food sometimes. He told me to never tell my aunt. I asked him why, and he said because she might make him stop bringing food over. So, I never said a thing.

"Then one day this nigga asked me to sit on his lap. Now, on some real shit, my father and I had had talks about boys, but he never went really far into details. So, I was a little confused about his intentions, and somehow, I felt trapped. And sure enough, as soon as I sat on his lap, he started asking dumbass questions and feeling on my legs.

"I jumped straight up, ran into another room, and locked the door. I thought, *Fuck this. I'm telling my aunt ASAP,* but that was a waste of time. She told me that I was probably being hot in the ass, and she didn't know why I was acting like that because she told me that I might have to put something together anyway.

"I thought, *So that's what she meant by that.* She was basically saying that fucking for food was an option of getting by.

"I'm not going to lie to you. I was scared to death. Every night I was hoping he didn't come by, hungry and all. Then one night, out of nowhere, I woke up to this nigga standing over top of me. I thought, *What the fuck?*

"He tried to talk me into taking my clothes off, and I told him no. Then he got mad and tried to forcefully undress me. Man, I spazzed out. I started yelling and kicking my legs hard as fuck. And luckily, one of those kicks caught his ass real hard in the nose. It must have been crazy hard, too, because this nigga fell to the ground, screaming like he was dying.

"My aunt came running in. Now, I know she noticed some of my clothes torn off me, but she said, 'Girl. What in the fuck did you do to him?'

"I couldn't believe she said that. I didn't know the first place to go, but at that moment I knew that it was time for me to go. I grabbed what little shit I had, stashed it in some bags, and bounced."

Chapter Ten

The Streets Made Me Cold

"I couldn't believe it. At the age of thirteen, I was homeless. I never did so much walking in my life. I became very familiar with all the parks. So familiar that I would take naps there. At night I slept in my aunt's building whenever I could get in.

"I became accustomed to the streets really fast. You had to sleep in public places like parks, where people were, for your safety. And at night you had to stay awake and keep moving. The streets were crazy and mad disrespectful. So, I had to become the streets. But I had to be a little messier than the streets because I was a female, and niggas thought shit was sweet. I stumbled across a nice blade one day in an alley, so I kept that on me.

"For my food, I either stole or stood around places where food was and looked hungry. A lot of times people would feel sorry for me and give me money or food. One thing I never did was beg for food or money. Not unless you call holding a sign up for food begging. I just never personally begged by mouth. And nigga, I never ate shit from the trash cans, asshole."

I pulled the blankets over my head and turned on my side.

"I never talked to anybody. If I did, it was most likely curse words. Now, as far as washing my ass goes, I did what I could do when I could. I copped book bags. I used them for my clothes and cosmetics. I used public places like hospitals, libraries, restaurants, etc., to take baths when I could. I kept brushing my teeth. It reminded me of my father. He was strict about teeth, and he was the funniest when he taught me.

"Anyway, I met this homeless lady that was cool as fuck. I could never understand why she was living in the streets because she was crazy smart. Her name was Brenda, but she asked me to call her 'Mrs. B.' Straight hood. Disrespect a bitch ASAP. She called me 'L'il Sis.' She hated the fact that I was so young and homeless.

"Like I said, I didn't do a lot of talking, but her ass talked nonstop. Mostly about the streets and how men were no good. She taught me some real-live shit though. She didn't want me to, but I hung out with her for weeks. Mrs. B wasn't the type who slept on the streets. She preferred inside places like train stations, hospitals, and sometimes, abandoned buildings.

"I quickly became an advantage for her, because I was so young that people almost instantly felt sorry for me and gave me money or bought me food. So, you know I would hit her off. She had a nice hustle game as well. Mrs. B could sing.

I mean, sing her ass off. I used to think, *What happened to this woman?* She was crazy smart and could sing. It just didn't make sense.

"She had this favorite spot downtown in the subway, where she would sing to make her money. One of her favorite songs was 'A Change Is Gonna Come' by Sam Cooke. She would literally have people in tears. Yo, B felt like family. I mean, real, genuine family.

"She asked me about my parents, I guess hoping she knew them, but when I told her that they were both deceased, she gave me this strange look and shook her head.

"This one day was a little different. We started moving a little earlier than normal. She took me to this one spot, sort of out of the way. When we reached the block, she told me to stand in front of this food spot while she went across the street. I was a little puzzled but paid it no mind.

"Anyway, when she got across the street, I saw her talking to this white woman and man. I was like, *What the hell?* Especially when I saw they kept looking back at me. When she came back over, I asked her what that was about, and she said that they were talking to her about a singing contract. I was like, 'That's good, Mrs. B.' I got excited for her."

"So, what happened?" I asked.

"She was like, 'They going to get back with me. Real shit, she was acting mad strange. She wasn't herself or excited about an opportunity for a contract.

"For the rest of the day it seemed like it was all positive talk about being successful. Then we put a nice meal together.

"The next morning, I was awakened by three people standing over me. I was like, 'Yo? What the fuck!' I yelled for Mrs. B, but she wasn't there. This big black security guard grabbed my arm. Then this little white woman said, "Young lady, my name is Mary, and I'm from the Division of Child Services. From what I heard, you've been living on the streets for a few weeks now, and you are too young to be living on your own. So we are here to put you in a better place."

"I yelled again, 'Yo, Mrs. B! Yo, let my fucking arm go. I don't need yo help. I live with my aunt Mickey.' I yelled again, 'Mrs. B!'

"They weren't trying to hear that shit. They manhandled my little ass and straight-up threw me in the car. I was mad as shit with Mrs. B. She had set me up.

"They took me to this place called Seamen's Societies for Children. I tell you, my mind was all over the place. One thing after another. Left home, moved in with my aunt, then the streets, and now, a foster home. All in a period of a few months."

Chapter Eleven

THE FOSTER HOME

"When I first got there, they took me to this office inside the building. It must have been lunchtime because there were a lot of kids in this one room that were loud as fuck. When we entered the office, there was this black lady named Latoya who introduced herself. She asked me my name, and I told her.

"She didn't waste no time. She laid down all the house rules. The hours for breakfast, lunch, dinner, and some other shit that flew by me. She also told me that my counselor's name was Ronnette. She said that if I had any questions or concerns, I could ask her in the morning.

"I was confused as shit. I was sitting in the chair, looking around. Then she started talking to the people who had brought me there. After they were done talking, she grabbed my hand and said, 'Follow me.' She took me to this closet that had netted laundry bags containing towels, face cloths, soap, deodorant, toothpaste, underwear, and socks. There were two sweat suits inside, and she gave me one. Then she walked me to the room where everyone was eating, to introduce me. There were four staff in the room. Two men and two women.

'Hi, everyone. This is Princess, and she will be staying here with us for a while.'

"The next thing you heard were smartass remarks. 'Princess, where is your crown?' 'You don't look like a princess.' 'We not trying to hear that; go sit down," and so on. Latoya said, 'Come on, y'all. Be nice.'

"It was both girls and boys eating together so I was a little confused until she explained where the boys stayed. This place was like a sectional spot. An east and west wing. The boys stayed on the west side. The sectionals were completely separated from each other unless it was lunch or recreation. But that didn't stop those niggas from being nasty. They were still sneaking from wing to wing, fucking. Shit, there were a few girls walking around with big bellies.

"Three months passed, and I became very familiar with my counselor, Ronnette. She was nice and gave me some good advice. She even set me up with this meeting where families came in to see if they wanted to adopt you. Shit, there were a few meetings I had, but nobody wanted me. I guess I always looked mean and made them feel like I had the potential of being a problem child.

"Ronnette would always tell me, 'You gotta smile and look happy. Don't you want to leave here, have a family, people who care about you, and a house to live in?' I mean, I felt where she was coming from, but I still wasn't over my father.

I knew he was dead, but I still wanted him back. I couldn't think of a life without having him in it.

"I could still hear her talking, but I drifted off slowly into a deeper reality. *This is real. I am all by myself.* The only family I had was Aunt Mickey, but she didn't act like it. I did tell Ronnette about my aunt, and she said that she would be contacting her regarding me. I told her, 'She doesn't even take care of her own kids, but it's up to you.'

"After that conversation, I felt a little depressed, so I went upstairs to lie down. I just lay on the bed and thought about some of the time my father and I had spent together. I missed the story telling and all the extra bubbles he would put in my bathwater. Thinking that, I thought maybe that would relax me a little—a nice hot bath. So, I grabbed my stuff. I filled the tub up, then got in and relaxed. I just didn't have all the bubbles.

"Everything was good until one of the girls who didn't like me came in there, starting trouble. Her name was Tina. Short, brown-skinned girl. She and a gang of bitches couldn't stand me. I honestly didn't know why and truly didn't give a fuck.

"She walked over to the tub, 'Bitch, talk that shit now.'

"I looked up at her. 'What the fuck are you talking about?'

"Then she made up some lie. 'Bitch, don't play dumb. You was talking all that shit; talk it now.'

"The first thing I tried to do was get out the tub, but she ran over and grabbed my hair, causing me to lose my balance. She started punching me in the face. I tried to swing back but kept slipping. Slipping so bad that I was going under the water. Then I felt her hand holding me under. I thought, *What the fuck? This bitch is trying to drown me.*

"I fought my way back up. When I came out of the water, I swung my head from side to side, clearing my vision. Right before she pushed me back under, I saw like four other people in the bathroom. Yo, I straight up panicked. It was like my life was flashing before my eyes. I started seeing childhood memories of my mother and father. This shit was crazy. Then, out of nowhere, I felt myself being snatched completely out of the water.

"It was Bruce. One of the security guards. He covered me with a towel. He didn't know what to do after that. I just lay there, coughing and fighting for my breath. A few seconds later, Mrs. Carrie and Mrs. Juanita, the other two staff, came running in, screaming, 'What happened?' They called the ambulance, but by the time it arrived, I was good. A nurse that worked there named Shala assisted me with CPR.

"Tina and the other girls who were involved were put on some type of sanctions for two months. One was they weren't allowed any recreation, and I'm not sure what the other one was.

"Anyway, time passed, and things were still the same with those bitches. I got into four fights. Two of them, I got jumped. The last fight was pretty bad because I was jumped by a gang of bitches, but there was this one dude that came busting into the middle of the fight, throwing the whores off me like rag dolls.

"He was like, 'Yo. What the fuck is wrong with you? You keep fucking with this girl for nothing. Fall the fuck back.

You keep fucking with her, I'm going to start winging. I don't give a fuck if you're male or female.'

"Yo, I looked up at this nigga, and he was in a rage. He grabbed my hand to lift me up. 'Get the fuck up. I'm only looking out because you not no scared bitch. You got heart. I'm just making that clear.'

"Then he walked away."

Chapter Twelve

TELL ME WHAT HAPPENED!!!!

I knew she was recovering, so I had never asked May what really happened the night she was shot. I was afraid that it would traumatize her. But the way she was talking, I didn't waste no time.

"Yo, May, I'm not trying to cut you off, but you got me wide awake. So, you might as well tell me what happened the night you got shot."

"Damn, nigga. I was in the middle of telling you some real shit."

"Yo, I feel you, but I really need to know. As a matter of fact, I been wanting to ask you this from day one."

"Why?"

"Because I want to know."

"Nigga, you probably thinking about doing some dumb shit."

"Man, I'm not thinking about doing nothing crazy. You going to tell me or what?"

She lay back on the bed, closed her eyes, and began telling me.

"Well, that day you had the music turned up loud and had me locked out of the room, I was trying to tell you where I was going. When I left your crib, I shot over to the Bronx, looking for Hector. Of course, the nigga is never really hard to find. Anyway, I found his ass in the middle of some crowd, talking shit. I stood outside the crowd until it cleared a little, then stuck my head in. It took a minute before anyone noticed me.

"Then some dude said, 'Yo. Who the fuck is you?'

"I was like, 'Why, nigga?'

'Bitch, because you in my circle, and you in my fucking hood.'

'Yo, fuck all that dumb shit you talking. I'm here to see my people.'

"He balled his fist and cocked back like he was about to swing. Then I heard a voice.

'Yo, nigga, chill. That gotta be May. But not looking like that.'

"Then he came and stood in front of me, 'Damn, girl. I can't believe this shit. You got your weight up and are looking good as fuck.'

"He went on and on for like five minutes. Then he partially introduced me to his boys. After that he pulled me to the side and asked me what was up with me.

"I gave him a brief story about you and me, then told him about what happened.

"Acting like he was concerned, he said, 'Yo, that's fucked up. What can I do to help?'

'I need to make some money really fast. No little shit, nigga.'

'Like what?'

'At least twenty racks.'

"Nigga took his hat off. 'Twenty racks. Yo, it's like I'm talking to a stranger.'

'Well, I'm not a stranger, nigga, you know that. But shit changed. I'm on some real shit now.'

"The whole time we were talking, his boys were ear hustling.

"He was like, 'Damn, this is crazy as fuck, because I got some big shit going down tonight. And I can use you.'

'Get the fuck outta here. You serious?'

'I'm dead serious. Hit me around seven tonight.'

'Okay, I'm down.'

"As soon as seven came, I hit him. He said that he had a big drop to make but never told me what it was. Then I remembered when you said something about the bags being heavy and him working me out of money. So, now I was pretty much sure it was coke, but shit, I didn't care. I was just trying to get paid.

"He said that the drop was going to take place in Brooklyn around eight that night and all I had to do was give the connect the money. That was it.

"I looked at him with a serious look. 'Nigga, all I have to do is pass some fucking money off for twenty racks?'

'Yo, bitch. Have I ever stood you wrong? No, I haven't. There's a reason for this shit.'

"Then he walked real close to me and looked me in the face. 'Yo, you got me or what?'

"I'm not going to front. I done a lot of shit for this nigga, and nothing never went wrong, but for some reason, that day I was feeling some kind of way. Sort of laughing, I gave him a slight punch to the chest and said, 'Yo, nigga, let's do this shit.'

"All that kept running through my mind was getting this money for us. I had never seen you so down like that, and it bothered me.

"Anyway, the drop came quick. Hector and like three of his boys were all in one car. We drove to some street that had a few cars on it.

"Hector parked in the middle of the block and said, 'Yo, take this bag and walk to the very top of the block. The second car from the stop sign, walk up to it and get in the back seat.'

"I got out of the car and looked at him. 'Yo, nigga, I swear, you better not be on no funny shit.'

"He handed me the bag. 'Here, man. Stop talking dumb.'

"The whole thing felt crazy strange, but I went with the flow anyway.

"When I got to the car, it had dark-tinted windows. I go hard, so I was like, *Fuck it.* I opened the back door and got in. There were three Mexicans in the car. Two up front and one sitting beside me. Nobody said a word. The guy beside me took the bag and started going through it. Then he started yelling at me in Spanish. I was like, 'Yo, what the fuck is going on?'

"Then he looked at me and started throwing the money back at me. Well, at least I thought it was, but it was very little money, mixed with cardboard and newspaper. Then, out of nowhere. the guy in the front passenger seat yelled, 'Bitch, this is what's going on!'

"Then he shot me. I wasn't sure where I was shot. All I saw was a gun pointed at me, then a loud sound. What's crazy was I was just sitting there until I noticed the guy next to me reach across to open my door, then push me out of the car. I don't really remember too much more after that besides waking up in the hospital, in pain."

"Damn, May. I told you about that dude."

"I know, nigga, but I been making runs for him all my life, and he never pulled no stunt like that."

Then I thought about the one story the boy told me. It was somewhat right, but somebody had also made up some shit. After hearing all this, it made me even more furious. This dude was too much and had been getting away with doing grimy shit for far too long. Something definitely had to be done.

"Yo, May, I appreciate everything. I just wish it wouldn't have happened like this."

And then I asked her, "How in the fuck did you meet up with this wack-ass clown anyway?"

Chapter Thirteen

MY FRIEND

"Like I was telling you before you cut me off, dummy. The dude that pulled the girls off me was Hector. After that, it seemed like he was always looking out for me. In that place they didn't feed you like shit. I felt like I was eating better on the streets.

"Yo, the boy was a slick talker and an amazing thief. His crazy ass would climb like four stories down to steal food out of the kitchen, then sneak his way back up.

"Anyway, he would hit me with food all the time. I know he had to think I was strange as fuck because I would never say nothing and would barely say thank you. But he knew I was thankful because I would grab that shit up quick. But shit, I thought he was strange too. Even though we were young, he wasn't on no funny shit like trying to fuck. I just know he didn't know me well enough to care about me. So, I was confused as fuck. He just always made sure I was straight.

"Then one day, shit changed dramatically. The EPA condemned the foster home due to asbestos in the walls. So, they started moving us out right away. I'm not sure where they moved Hector, but they moved me to this shithole spot. There were no boundaries there, and you could basically go and come as you pleased. I was definitely not comfortable sleeping there because, somehow, grown-ass people would sneak inside. Security was wack.

"Before Hector left, he gave me a letter with his info on it. He wrote that he wasn't doing the foster home anymore and that he was going to stay with his aunt in the Bronx. And if that didn't work out, then he would be at his grandma's spot in Harlem. He also wrote that if I needed anything, I should call him. I stashed his info away in this little purse I bought on the street.

"I knew that Hector was strange, but honestly, he was the only friend that I had besides Mrs. B. I did ask him one day at the foster home why he was there. He told me that both of his parents were strung out on drugs. And one day, the state found him abandoned in their home. He said that he was left alone for three days with no food. When he told me that, I then realized that there were a lot of people out there that are fucked up too.

"To me, at the time, he was good people. I felt a little different about him after that story. I still couldn't put it together why he got so attached to me. I know he said I had heart, but…

"Anyway, everything was so different then, and I knew that I couldn't do this for too long. This place was crazy. In the morning it was run like a foster home. You had your counselors and security guards. The counselors would bring in small amounts of inexpensive food that you would have to cook yourself. It was mostly cereal and milk for breakfast, and for lunch and dinner it was always dollar frozen dinners.

"As for night, or should I say after the counselors left, shit got weird. During the night you could hear people walking around. Sometimes you could hear different voices talking too. On some real shit, I think the guards were selling drugs to the junkies. There were six girls to a room. We kept our door locked and barricaded.

"The whole place was a big scam. They just needed kids to keep the place running. And that wasn't going to last too long, 'cause kids were leaving every day.

"So, I went with the flow for about two weeks, then I decided to leave. Wasn't no future there, and I started feeling hopeless. I knew my aunt Mickey wasn't shit, but I had to be a part of something. A nice long week on the streets, and I found my way back to the hellhole."

Chapter Fourteen

BACK TO THE HELLHOLE

"So, I made my way back to the hellhole. Her apartment was on the sixth floor. Once you got off the elevator, you made a right, and her apartment was four doors down on the left. When you walked into her apartment, to the immediate right was the kitchen. The kitchen had a second entrance connecting to the dining room. And the dining room was a joint connection with the living room.

"Now, if you walked straight in instead of going into the kitchen, there was the master bedroom on the left, followed by a bathroom and then another bedroom. The apartment had a nice size to it, but being as though it was always junkie and dirty, it looked small. The living room had a two-piece sofa set that was in poor condition and a table with only two chairs. Now, look, I'm not going to front because I know sometimes it can be a real struggle coming up. But seriously, you could easily tell that she wasn't trying.

"As far as the kids, like I was saying, she had eight, but only four lived with her, the two boys, ages eight and six, and the two girls, four and two. Daron was the oldest, then Kevin, Yasmine, and Tajah. On some real shit, the kids weren't really all that bad. The two boys, all they knew was their Nintendo until they got hungry. The oldest girl was a little sassy and didn't know how to take no for an answer. But she couldn't help it. She got that shit from her momma. The baby never really cried. She was a good baby.

"Anyway, when I walked in, nobody but the kids were there, including the baby. I thought, *Babies watching babies.* The house was crazy junky. Shit was everywhere. As a matter of fact, I didn't need to knock to get in because the door was partially open.

"I figured I would try to straighten the house a little. I did, but it didn't really make too much of a difference. However, I did notice a brand-new fifty-inch flatscreen. I thought I knew where that came from. She either fucked for it or owed somebody.

"I sat there until she finally made it in. I was sleepy, so I was stretched out on the couch.

"She came in all loud, 'Who the fuck is that on my couch?'

"I sat up. 'It's me, Princess.'

'Who the hell told you to come back?'

"I responded softly, 'I didn't have anywhere else to go.'

'So, where the fuck you been?'

"I was thinking in my head the whole time, *Why the fuck you cuss so much?*

'I been living on streets and in the foster home.'

'Ever since you pulled that little stunt with my boyfriend, you left, then he left.'

"I thought to myself, *I know she's not accusing me of being or living with her boyfriend.* She just kept on talking. Then she said, 'If you plan on staying here, you are going to watch these kids and keep this house clean.' And then she said, 'And if you don't do a good job doing it, you can take your ass right back with that nigga.'

"I snapped, 'Aunt Mickey, I wasn't with that fucking clown.'

'Oh, you grown now. Who the fuck you cussing at?'

'Not you. I'm talking about him.'

"She was like, 'Whatever, just do what I said.'

"I did what I had to do. I took care of the kids and the house. And it was a lot. I was inexperienced when it came to taking care of kids because I never had to before. Now, as far as cooking went, I only cooked small stuff. However, I did become a little creative when my father got sick. I would try to cook chicken, but it never seemed to turn out right. My mac and cheese, rice, and stuffing didn't turn out too bad. I mainly cooked hot dogs, noodles, eggs; you know. Small shit. So, in a way, I could halfway feed their asses. But that was only if there was food to cook every day.

"She did supply food for them, but very little. She would always complain about the food being eaten too quickly, and honestly, I would stretch the food so much that the kids would still be crying hungry after I fed them.

"I remember when I was living on the streets, I would always see these people standing in line, waiting on free food. Sometimes I would see them walk away with two or three bags.

"One day the kids were crying because they were hungry and kept asking me for food. So, I said, 'Fuck it. Let me try this spot out.' I told Yasmine to watch the baby. I told her not to take the baby out of the playpen and not to open the door for anybody until I got back. Yo, I know that shit was crazy because they were both babies, but I had to take the boys to help me with the bags. The two girls would have made it difficult. The place was only about ten minutes away, but how long the line was going to be was my concern.

"Anyway, I had to make a move, so I grabbed the two boys and made my way over there. Just as I thought, the line was long, but it was moving pretty quickly. When we reached the top of the line, there were four people making bags.

"One lady asked, 'Hey, you're young. Where are your parents?'

"She caught me off guard. I really didn't know what to say. And at the same time, I didn't want my dumbass aunt to get in trouble. So, I made up some shit, 'She's home sick.'

"Then, out of nowhere, the oldest boy, Daron, spoke up. 'And we're hungry.'

"The lady was very nice and awfully concerned. She had this cart behind her and as she was talking to me, she was filling it up. She gave us like two times the amount of food that they were supposed to give out. And we had bags to carry.

This woman knew something was wrong. I was sure of that. She sent us on our way, told us to be careful, and asked me if I would be kind enough to bring her cart back. My cold-ass ways that I had inherited over time wouldn't allow me to be passionate or show my appreciation. So, I was like, 'Okay,' and walked off.

"When we got back to the crib, both babies were crying. Look, I'm not good in situations like that. My life had been hell since my father died. I didn't have time for no soft shit.

"So, I yelled, 'Yo, you got to shut the fuck up. I'm about to cook for yo asses now. Shit.'

"They looked at me like, 'You shut the fuck up!' and went back to crying.

"Yo, I fried up some hot dogs and eggs for their asses. They were happy, and the crying stopped immediately. They gave us a lot of food. Powdered milk, eggs, canned food, cereal, frozen meat, a box of noodles, and other items. We were straight for a while. After I put everything away, I changed the baby and fell back on the couch to relax.

"Time went by and before you knew it, it was time to eat again. So, I fed them. Then, later, we took our baths and went to bed."

"Yo, Mike, I know you're probably thinking, 'Damn, where was the mom?'"

Mike answered, "Yeah. Where the fuck was she?"

"Mike, she was gone like two or three days sometimes."

"Yo, your aunt was mad messy. She didn't give a fuck about nothing."

"Yo, you think that's messy. Check out what happened next."

"Later that night, while I was asleep, she came in, drunk as fuck, talking about 'Your asses better be asleep, 'cause I got company.' The kids slept in one room. There wasn't enough room for me to sleep with them, so I slept on the couch. I didn't say anything; I just played asleep. Then I heard a loud smack, followed by a dude's voice, 'Damn, bitch. You came out of them clothes quick.'

"Almost tripping over her own damn feet, she moaned, 'Come on, nigga. Fuck me.'

"I had always heard of people fucking, but I had never seen it go down. She climbed onto the small sofa on her knees; he got behind her, and they started fucking. They were both crazy loud, her screaming and the dude talking loudly.

"I thought, *Shit, I ain't ever fucking.* That shit looked and sounded painful. Then my next thought was, *She's going to wake the kids up.* But on the other hand, the kids were probably used to that shit. That couldn't have been the first time.

"Yo, he held it on her ass for like twenty minutes straight. Then he yelled out, 'Yo! What the fuck?' Apparently, she had fallen asleep on his ass.

'Yo. Get the fuck back up here.'

"She didn't respond. She just lay there. It was almost like I could hear snoring.

'OK. You want to fall asleep on a nigga, do you?" He got down on his knees to reach the level she was now on. Then he started fucking her again.

"She woke up. 'Yo. Nigga, chill.'

'Nah, I'm chilling. You want to fall asleep on a nigga?'

"It went on for like another ten or twenty minutes, then she was right back out again. Then shit got crazy. When he was finished, he stood up and walked toward the door. Then I heard him say, 'Nigga, she's knocked out. Help yourself. And yo, make sure you lock the door when you're done.'

"I was scared as fuck. This dude was huge. Some big black nigga. He came in, looking all around the house, bedrooms and everything. Dude had the nerve to come stand over top of me. He didn't do nothing. He just stood there for a minute then walked off. He walked over to my aunt, snatched her up, and dragged her into the bedroom.

"Yo. I was afraid for her. It took me about five minutes to get enough heart up to move. When I got up, I walked over to the door. I stood there to listen but heard nothing. Then I went to the kids' room. I woke the two boys up. I told them to walk with me to go wake their mom up. The oldest said, almost in a crying voice, 'Why? What's wrong?'

'Yo. Be quiet. And come on.'

"I thought if the dude saw kids, he would get soft, feel bad, and run off. But right when we were about to walk out of the room, I heard the door open. He was walking around in the house for a few before he left. I told the boys to be quiet. I stayed in the room until I heard the front door close. I immediately ran and locked both locks on the door.

"Then I ran into the room where Aunt Mickey was. She was lying on her back, completely naked. I checked her thoroughly to make sure she was good and that she was breathing. Everything was good. I just covered her ass up and walked out.

"I told the boys to go back to bed. I thought the night was over, but then I noticed the fifty-inch flatscreen TV was gone."

Chapter Fifteen

WHERE IS THAT LETTER?

"The next day she woke up like nothing had happened, just walking around and making up shit to complain about. She went to the kitchen, I guess for something to drink, and noticed the food in the refrigerator. You would think that she should be grateful, but instead, she said, 'Where the fuck you get this shit at?'

"I was like, 'Why? I got it off the food line on 32nd.'

'Bitch. What you mean why? This is my shit, and you ain't going to just be bringing shit in here without me knowing it.'

'Well, the kids didn't have nothing to eat.'

'Stop lying, Princess; there was shit in there for them to eat.'

"Then she walked around the corner. 'Oh my God. Bitch, I know you didn't sell my TV for no fucking food.'

'No. I didn't.'

'Yo. For real. Where the fuck is my TV?'

‘You can ask the boys. They went with me to the food line.’

‘Look, this is my last time asking you. Where is my TV?’

‘Yo. The dude you bought home with you last night? His friend stole it.’

‘Bitch. Ain’t nobody come home with me last night.’

“Before I had a chance to say anything else, she hit me. She grabbed me by the hair and fucked me up for real. I tried to fight her back, but she was way too strong and big for me. She was an experienced fighter. That’s all she did. The bitch blacked both my eyes and swelled my face up. I did manage to get one good kick off. I kicked her knee backward while she was standing in front of me. It sounded like her shit broke. She fell to the ground, screaming, ‘I’m going to kill you, bitch!’

“The only thing I could think of was, *Back to the streets for me*. I grabbed my book bag, stuffed it with my clothes, and put the rest of my shit in bags. Then I walked back out to the living room. The kids watched all this dumb shit go on. I felt sorry for them. After being around them for about six months, they had grown on me.

“Yeah, my aunt was in pain, but she realized the pain of me leaving was worse. I was holding down shit in her crib. I kept the house clean and the kids fed. Now her ass had to do it. Shit, she was already whoring me, and now she was hitting on me. Nah, I wasn’t with that. I had to go. The kids were holding my legs and crying, not wanting me to leave.

“Adjusting my eyes, I looked at the oldest boy and said, ‘Hey. You got to take care of them. No soft shit, and stop crying. They're going to depend on you now. You know what to do. You hear me?'

"He looked at me, wiping his tears while moving his head in a 'yeah' like motion. The whole time this was taking place, she was trying to cop a plea for me to stay. I paid her ass no mind. The only thing that was running through my head was that this might be the last time I saw my little cousins. So, the next thing I said could possibly be a lie, but I had to say something.

"Walking out the door, I said, 'You be good. I'll be back.'

"Now I was right back on the streets again. I'd never felt so alone in my life. I made some of my old moves, but it was different now. It was damn near winter, and all my spots were too cold. So, I watched the other homeless people's moves. I followed some of them to warming centers. Those were places provided to the homeless so they could stay warm. But when you were moving and trying to make a hustle, the subway heating shafts were the move.

"My hustling game was getting me by. I just stood on the busiest street corners with a sign that read, 'Need food or money, please.' And people would put money in my can. Since I was making a little money, I would use some of it to travel around the city. Shit, it was something to do, and I started liking it. I was learning New York City, big time. I used money for cabs and trains, but mostly I preferred the trains. I looked rough, and them cab drivers were mad picky.

"The only thing about traveling too far away was that you always wanted to return to the spot where you felt comfortable sleeping, or you would find yourself in some uncomfortable situations. Speaking of uncomfortable. One day I was over in Manhattan, getting my hustle on. It was a good day for me. It seemed like everybody was hitting my can. As a matter of fact, it was the most I had ever made in a short period of time, I guessed because I was so young or because it was now snowing really bad.

"Anyway, they felt sorry for me. When living on the streets, it's very easy to tell who's a bum or a homeless person. I couldn't help but notice these two black men across the street, watching me. I kept catching them staring at me. They would walk off for like ten minutes and then meet up again in the same spot. I wasn't no dummy on the streets. And I paid close attention to shit. But I slipped on that one because of the weather.

"The snow started piling up quickly. It was coming down so hard that you could barely see. On top of the snow coming down, the temperature was now dropping significantly. My fucking feet were freezing, and I had to get somewhere to warm them up ASAP. I looked across the street, and the two men were gone. It was time to go. I stood up and stuffed my money away in my pockets. I went to the closest subway to warm up.

"The whole scenery at this subway was completely different from the one I was familiar with. This spot was rough. When a train stopped, the subway became crazy crowded, but in seconds, everyone vanished. No one was left but the homeless people.

"I saw this bench with this homeless lady sitting on it, so I figured I'd go have a seat next to her. I also noticed how dim the lights were in this subway. It seemed like they were going from dim to bright. Anyway, the lady that I was sitting next to got up and walked off. Then, out of nowhere—I mean it happened fast—the two dudes who were watching me from across the street when I was making money were now standing in front of me.

"I thought, *What the fuck?* I did have my blade, but I couldn't reach it fast enough. Yo, these dudes were scary as fuck. They just looked fucking crazy.

"The one that stood to the right of me had on these dirty, dark brown boots and wrinkled, stained blue jeans. It almost looked like he had two or three jeans on under the ones he was wearing. And he had this dark blue, ripped-up bomber jacket with cotton hanging out of it. I really couldn't see his face. He wasn't wearing a face mask, but it was something that covered the bottom part of his face, nose down. He had on a brown cotton hat that was partially covered by a dingy gray hoodie. His nose was running bad, because the mask nose area was wet.

"Now, I know for sure that the guy standing to my left was wearing extra clothes, because it was cold as shit out, and he had on these faded black track pants, tucked inside of some mismatched boots. This dude was a real-live bum. I did notice that he was wearing a black hat, but that was about it, because the dude to the right of me grabbed my leg. He snatched me off the bench violently. Then the guy to the left grabbed my arms. I started kicking like crazy.

"Mike, you know I got a nice kick game."

I was being smart. "Yeah, I know. That's how you been winning all your fights, May."

"Anyway, the dude to the right cocked his fist back and yelled, 'Bitch, if you kick me, I'm going to break your shit.'

"He put his knee over both my legs and used his weight to pin them down. Then he started searching through my pockets. While he was looking for money, the dude to the left was on some funny shit. He kept grabbing for my titties and my pussy. Now the crazy thing is that I was bundled up pretty good, so I didn't know what the fuck he was feeling for. He was just sick as fuck.

"None of this lasted long, because they knew that the next train was coming. When they ran off, the little bit of shit I had in my book bag was now scattered across the concrete. I was hot. They took all my money. I didn't even have money to catch the train back to Brooklyn.

"I just sat there, hopeless, and didn't know what to do. I thought, *I'm too young to be in these streets. I gotta do something, because shit like this can keep happening. Maybe even worse the next time.* Then it came to me, *Call Hector.* Then I thought, *Where is that letter?* I looked through my half-full bag in a frantic way, hoping that they didn't take my purse that didn't have shit in it.

"Thank God. My purse was still in my bag. I searched through my purse, and the letter was still there. However, they did go through it because it was open. I was like, *Good. Now all I have to do is make some money to get back to Brooklyn.*

"After I warmed up a little, I went back to the streets to try to hustle up some money. The snow had come down something serious, and there were a lot fewer people on the streets. However, I did manage to make a quick twenty dollars. I caught the train back to Brooklyn, and I grabbed something to eat along the way. I went to my spot around the people I knew and crashed out.

"Early the next morning, I went to my favorite restaurant to brush my teeth and wash my ass. It wasn't a public restroom. The people who owned it would let me use it from time to time as long as I kept it clean. When I got done, I went to a pay phone to call Hector but got no answer. So, I grabbed something to eat. About a half hour later, I tried again. This time I got an answer.

'Hola.'

'Hello. Is Hector there?'

"It was a lady who answered. She put the phone down and started yelling in Spanish. Then a dude's voice came over the phone, 'Yo.'

'What's up, nigga?'

'Who this?'

'It's Princess from the foster home.'

"He got hype. 'Yo. What the fuck? What up with you?'

'Nothing. Shit's fucked up. I'm back on the streets again, nigga.'

'Nah. What happened?'

'The one foster home they sent me to was a real shithole. So, I left to go live with my aunt. Then she got on some nut shit, and I left.'

'Yo. Come the fuck over here. I got a spot for you.'

'That's what's up, because shit is crazy over here, yo.'

'I mean, you can't stay with me, 'cause my aunt's crazy as fuck. But I got a spot for you.'

'Yo. It got to be better than living on the streets.'

'I mean it's my uncle's trap spot. Believe me, nobody's going to fuck with you. We don't play no crazy shit over here. I'll plug you in, so don't worry.'

'Nigga, I'm not worried about nothing.'

'My bad. I forgot. The bitch with mad heart.'

'Yeah, I hear. When can I come?'

'I don't care. Shit, you can come today if you want.'

"We talked a little longer on the phone. He gave me his info and told me a good time to catch him on the block."

Chapter Sixteen

SPANISH FLY

"Hector lived in the Bronx, East Tremont. I knew nothing about this neighborhood. Spanish people were everywhere. Yo. I felt so out of place. I mean, I had been in a lot of different neighborhoods, but the races were always mixed. Most of the time. I'm just saying, all I heard was people speaking Spanish. But it was all good. Nobody was fucking with me.

"I went to the specific location where he said he would be, but I didn't see him. The spot he was talking about had like eight dudes standing there. So, I walked across the street to the corner store and stood there, hoping to see him sometime soon. I didn't want to be standing too long. People would eventually notice me and think I was on some snake shit.

"Not even ten minutes later, guess who walked out of the corner store? I was standing right in front of him, and he didn't even notice me. Nigga walked right by me, eating his sandwich.

"I ran up on him. 'Yo. Hector.'

"He turned around and looked at me. Still chewing his food, he said, 'Yoooo. What's good? I see you made it. I thought you was bullshitting.'

'Nigga, I do no bullshitting.'

"He started laughing. 'Shit, it's all good. Let me introduce you to my people. Come on.' This dude didn't waste no time. Shit was crazy, because he was acting like he really missed me or something.

"Hector was a frail, high-yellow Latino with silky black hair and light brown eyes. It looked like he had put on a little weight though. I didn't know what he was like on the streets. I mean, to be honest, I didn't know what he was like in the foster home either. But I didn't give a fuck. I mean, after all, the nigga did look out for me. Besides, I didn't have nothing to lose by checking him out.

"Anyway, we went across the street to where those dudes were. Hector introduced me as his little Tata. I didn't, and I still don't understand why he called me that. And I never cared to ask. But that became my new name for a while. His boys kept giving crazy little looks. They acted like they didn't want to, but they spoke, 'Yo. What up, Tata?'

"So, you know me. I don't do a lot of talking. I just gave them the head nod. After that I just spent the rest of the day meeting people Hector knew. When it started getting late, we went to this restaurant his family owned and ate.

"While we were eating, he told me, 'Yo, check this. You can't come live with me because my auntie be tripping, but my people own a few trap houses you can chill at. We going to go by a few of them to see if I can squeeze you in. Now, if everything goes right, we going to get you cleaned up so you can start making some money.'

"I gave that nigga a crazy look. 'Yo, Hector. What you mean by that? Because I'm not trying to be on no whoring shit.'

'Nah, man. Ain't nobody on that type of time. You probably be running errands or some shit.' Then he just gave me this stupid look and kept walking.

"After we were done eating, we shot to these apartments. The apartments had these black gates that surrounded them. Once you walked through the gates, there were big glass doors for the entrance of the building. People were all out front by the gates and standing by the glass doors. It was almost like they were guarding the building.

"It seemed Hector know everyone because he was getting mad love from everybody. Somebody was coming out of the building and held the door open for us. The apartment we were going to was on the twelfth floor, F-16. We caught the elevator up. When we got to the door, Hector did this strange knock, then started speaking in Spanish. Then some old man opened the door.

"Pretty much after that, I didn't know what was going on or what was being said. All I know is that Hector kept looking back at me, pointing. This went on for like twenty minutes. I was just standing there. One thing I found out about Spanish people is that they love hard. If you're a part of the family in any kind of way, you're loved unconditionally. Whatever Hector said must have convinced the old man, but it didn't come easy.

"The old man looked at me and said, 'Hi, little lady. What's your name?'

"He surprised the shit out of me. I didn't think he spoke English. Even though his English was very terrible, I still understood him. Before I had a chance to answer, Hector spoke.

'Uncle José, her name is Tata.'

"He took two steps past Hector, 'Hey. She speak.'

"I stood, looking confused, 'I guess Tata. I mean, that's what he called me.'

"The uncle smiled with all his fronts missing and said, 'Tata, welcome to my home. You stay there.'

"He pointed to this room. Then Hector walked over to open the door. The room was small and had a twin bed in it. The walls were in bad shape. A lot of paint was missing from them. The room wasn't crazy junky, but there was trash scattered around.

"Hector walked into the room then turned around and looked at me, 'Yo, look, Tata, he said you could stay here for a couple months or until you get yourself together, but that's it. He said just help him out around the house with a few things.' Then he paused and gave me this serious look. 'Yo, look. The kitchen is off-limits because it be some shit in there. So, if you need to use it, just let him know.'

"Staring back at him, I whispered, 'What shit, nigga?'

"He was like, 'Tata, you good. It don't have shit to do with you. Just be happy you got somewhere to chill.'

"Setting my bags on the floor, I said, 'Nigga, I'm happy. I just don't have no time for no crazy shit.'

"Hector was now walking out the door. 'You good, Tata. I got you. My folks are good people. No harm will come your way.'

"When he said that, I was a little leery, but in the same sense, I believed him. He talked to his uncle a little longer, then told me he would see me in the morning.

"The apartment had two small bedrooms. When you walked in, the bathroom was to your left, and the kitchen was to your right. The two bedrooms were like right next to each other. The setup was just like my aunt Mickey's spot. The living room was connected to the kitchen. He had a little box TV sitting on the stand and an old-school wood sofa set. You know, the type that has the brown flowers on it.

"His kitchen table was old too. I'm thinking he had to have been living there for a long time. For one, the old-ass furniture and two, the old scent of the house. The apartment smelled like old wood, with a loud scent of Vick's Rub.

"Anyway, it was getting late. Nobody was there but the old man in the living room. I wasn't feeling any of this, but it beat living in the streets. On top of that, I was tired as shit and was ready to take it down. I checked the door to see if it had a lock on it, and it did. So, I locked myself in and moved the bed against the door.

"Moving the bed revealed even more trash. Old Snapple tea bottles with tea still inside them, mixed with who knows what. Used condoms, cigarette butts, blunt wrappers, loose change. I mean all kinds of shit.

"I just sat on the bed with my feet pulled to the backs of my thighs and thought about my father. I remember he used to tell me, 'Baby, it's a big world out there. You're going to face good times and bad times.' I was too young to take what he was saying seriously. Most of the time I would laugh and give him a big kiss and hug. But damn, now I saw what he meant. Shit was fucked up with me. I was thinking, *Well, shit, where are the good times?* I just sat there and thought about happy moments. I was truly in my happy place.

"The next morning came quick. It was loud as shit in the apartment. It sounded like twenty people were in the living room. I mean, the sounds could have easily been mistaken for arguing. I was scared as shit for a minute. I had to use the bathroom bad, but I didn't feel comfortable walking out there. Then, right when I was thinking about trying to piss in one of the bottles on the floor, I heard a knock on the door.

"Not sure who it was, I answered with a tough voice, 'Yo.'

'Yo, Tata, open up. It's me, Hector.'

"I thought, *Damn. I thought I heard his voice.* Even though it was in Spanish.

"I was like, 'All right. Hold on.'

"When I opened the door, he barged in. 'Yo. Why you barricaded in here?'

Then he started laughing. 'Damn, I told you, my people aren't on any funny shit. Even though they're mad as shit that you're up in here.'

"Then he started laughing again. I wasn't paying his ass any mind. All I was thinking about was how bad I had to piss. He had a brown bag that had some food in it. He gave it to me. I set it on the bed. I told him thanks but said I needed to go to the bathroom ASAP.

"He was like, 'Well, go to the bathroom then.'

"I grabbed my book bag and shot out of the room to go to the bathroom. Shit, there were like ten motherfuckers in the apartment. Most of them were in the kitchen. Two of them were standing over the stove, cooking something. At the time, I didn't know exactly what they were cooking. And four other people were standing around the kitchen table, counting money. Yo, there were piles of money on the table. Everyone else was standing in the living room, staring out the windows. I instantly thought, *What the fuck?*

"When I went into the bathroom, it was clean. Well organized. I couldn't believe it, what with all those people. Inside my book bag I had enough stuff to take a decent shower, but I didn't comfortable doing so with all those people being here. I thought, *I'll just wait until tonight.* So, I just took a quick wash and brushed my teeth. After that I went back to the room.

"Hector came into the room with me to buss it up a little while I ate my sandwich. Then someone came into the room after a brief knock. He was a tall, light-skinned Hispanic.

This guy had to be the boss. I mean, everything got quiet, and he did all the talking. Every individual spoke separately when speaking to him. Even Hector stood quietly in the doorway.

"After the boss got his point across, everyone went back to talking, but not as loud as they were before he came in. This was crazy because he was standing in the room, talking to people outside the room. I felt that to be a little awkward. I was just sitting there, eating my sandwich on the bed. Then he walked over to Hector.

"He was wearing boots, blue jeans, a fitted Yankees hat, and a black leather jacket that had a strong leather scent. It was almost like he had just bought the jacket. Surprisingly, he spoke pretty good English.

'So, Hector, introduce me to our new friend.'

'Oh. Uncle Sebo, this is Tata. I met her when I was in foster care. She's real good people, Unc, and I'm trying to look out for her because she has no place to go. She's been living on the street.'

"Then he walked over to me. 'Hello, Tata, my name is Sebo, and from my understanding, you don't have a place to live. So, you're hoping you can stay here for a while. Am I correct?'

"Now, you know that my communication skills are terrible, but there was something about this dude. His demeanor and the way he presented himself almost put me in mind of my father.

"So, I said an instant response that even surprised me. 'Yes. I was hoping I could.'

"Hector looked at me in surprise.

"Still looking at me, Sebo asked, 'Well, would you be nice enough to help my papi out around the house and run some errands for him?'

"Then I got a little hood. 'Yeah, I guess I can do that.'

'Okay. It's not much. Just keeping the house clean, grabbing his food from the store and his medication from the pharmacy. He eats out during the day, because the kitchen is off-limits from eight to six. What goes on in here is never to be talked about on the streets. That is very important for you to know. We take loyalty very seriously around here. Life or death, seriously. You understand me?'

"Then I got soft again. 'Yes. I understand you.'

"He held his hand out so I could shake it. I did. Then he said, 'Welcome to the family. Hey. Tata, if you don't mind me asking. Where are your parents?'

"Letting go of his hand, I sat back on the bed. 'Both of my parents are dead.'

"He just gave me this strange look. 'Oh, Tata, I'm sorry to hear that.'

"What was strange was right after I said that, he gave Hector this strange look as well. He walked over, gave Hector a hug, and whispered loud enough that I could hear it, 'Hey, take this and take her shopping. She doesn't look like she has much.' Then he told Hector that he had somewhere to be.

"Sebo looked back at me. 'I'll see you around, little lady.'

"I didn't say anything. I just lifted my head to say bye.

"It seemed like everybody had somewhere to be all at the same time, because everyone left at the same time. Shit. In less than five minutes, everybody was gone except Pop. I found out real quick that Pop had a favorite chair he sat in, right next to the window. I guess he liked looking at the sky or the view of other buildings, because he damn sure couldn't see the streets or cars. The apartment floor was too far up.

"He was a dark-skinned Dominican. It looked like he could have been in his seventies. He walked really slow and had a slight hunch in his back. Hector asked him if he was okay and if he was hungry. He said that he was fine, but he had some prescriptions at the pharmacy and wanted to know if Hector would grab them for him. Hector told him yeah, and we left."

Chapter Seventeen

WELCOME TO THE FAMILY

"So, we left the apartment and made our way to the store. Along the way, Hector introduced me to the people he knew. He said that it was important for him to do that because people would respect me off the strength of him and his family. We went to like five different stores.

"Hector kind of ran the show. But I did have some say. I don't know exactly how much Sebo gave him, but I bought a lot of shit. Two pairs of sneaks, some boots, five different pairs of jeans, mad shirts, socks, panties, bras, cosmetics. Shit, I was straight.

"But on some real shit, I couldn't stop thinking about what was going on here. I mean, nobody does that kind of shit for nothing, plus giving me a place to stay. Something was going on, and this nigga wasn't telling me. Anyway, the day flew by. We did a lot of walking, which I was very used to, and met a lot of people, which I didn't care so much about.

"When we got back to the apartment, it was well after six, so Pop was there by himself. While we were out, Hector had grabbed his meds and some rice and chicken from the corner store. Hector didn't stay long. He talked to Pop for a while, then told me that he'd see me in a few days. I wasn't sure what that was about. I just told him, 'Okay, I'll get with you then.'

"After he left, it got completely quiet. All you heard was the low sound of the *Price Is Right* game show that Pop was watching on TV. Pop had this small TV sitting on a stand damn near sitting right in front of him. All he did was watch TV. Sometimes he would watch some strange shit that didn't make no sense. Kind of hard to explain.

"I had all these bags with new shit in them, so I didn't want to bring them into a dirty room. It was after six, so I could go in the kitchen now. I grabbed a broom and some trash bags. I swept the room thoroughly and put all the trash in bags. I even found a bucket under the sink. I added some cleaning stuff to it and wiped the walls down.

"I had to admit. It started looking like a bedroom. Inside the room was a small closet. There weren't any hangers in there, so I just set my bags on the floor. I looked over at the bed and realized that I didn't have a sheet or blanket. I had a small blanket in my bag, but I really didn't want to use it. It was a little dirty from the streets. But shit, I was far from complaining. This was like paradise compared to the streets. As crazy as this might sound, I felt like I was good there.

"My next move was a nice hot shower. I hadn't had a nice shower since the foster home. Only wash-ups. I was good now.

Pop was the only one there, and I felt comfortable getting in the shower. Afterward, I threw away the clothes I had on. I thought, *Yes, a fresh start.* I told Pop that I would see him in the morning, and I took it down.

"Morning came fast, and I was once again awakened by a knock on the door. This time it wasn't Hector. It was Uncle Sebo.

"I got up and opened the door. 'Yo. What's up?'

'Good morning, Tata.'

"Standing there, still sleepy as hell, I didn't say nothing.

"He handed me a piece of paper with a list of items on it and told me that he needed them right away. I looked at him like, 'Nigga, I'm still trying to get my eyes fucking open.' Then he asked me some dumb shit that I kind of took offense to, but I let it slide.

'Tata, can you read?'

'What! Yeah, I can read. Why would you ask me that?'

'Ta, no disrespect, but there's a lot of people that can't read.'

'Well, I can. What's up?'

'I need you to run a few errands today. The stuff on this paper, I need right away. And as a matter of fact, I'm going to need the same exact items every morning by eight. Not on Sundays though. Also, Pop needs his breakfast by eight because he must eat before taking his meds. His lunch is at twelve, and his dinner is at four thirty.'

"Yo, I didn't know what the fuck to say. I mean, I know they were looking out for a bitch, but he was bussing up in here, demanding shit. I started to tell his bitch ass, 'Fuck you' and walk straight out, but then I thought, *Shit, I guess this is the way I pay my rent. But this dude needs to find a better fucking way of communicating. You don't wake nobody up early in the morning, demanding shit. I mean, I know I can't just lie up in this bitch, but this shit came too fast. Shit, I barely got my feet in the door.*

"Anyway, I told him, 'Yeah. I can handle that.'

"He was like, 'Hey, Ta, we got to take care of each other. You understand what I'm saying?' He must have noticed the attitude I had.

"Now, looking for my toothbrush, I said, 'Yo, dude, I get what you are saying.'

"I looked at the list, and there was strange shit on it. Well, at least I thought so at this time. He wanted ammonia, baking soda, plastic baggies, and some other shit. I was like, *This dude is strange.*

"I'm not going to front though. The more I took care of Pop, the more he took care of me. I didn't have to worry about nothing. I was straight. After three weeks, I had everything down pat. Pop was in good hands. Pop and I even built a good friend bond. He didn't talk much, and neither did I. We had our favorite talk shows that we watched every night together. He had pictures of his kids all around the house. I tried to ask him about the pictures, but he would look at me and then the picture and smile. Pop struggled with his English pretty bad. However, there were some words that I could make out.

"I'm not a people person, but running errands for Pop, I met a lot of people. Sebo told me that if I ever ran into any problems on the street, to let them know that I worked for him and I'd be good. Then he said, 'But not the cops.'

"On the flip side, I didn't see Hector at all. I asked Sebo about him a few times, but he would always tell me that he was doing some work for him. Then about two months passed, and Hector finally came around. He popped up at Pop's one evening. I'm not going to hold you. I was happy to see him.

"He gave me a big hug and said, 'I heard that you are fitting in really well.'

'Yeah. Everything been good.'

'That's what's up.'

"He walked over to Pop, gave him a hug, and then they started speaking in Spanish.

"After that we left to grab something to eat and walked around for a while. I know it almost sounds like Hector and I could have started kicking it, but Hector didn't look at me in that kind of way. He thought of me like one of his niggas off the street. On our way back to the crib, he told me that Sebo wanted him to show me a few drop-off locations.

"I was like, 'Drop-off locations? What the fuck are you talking about?'

'Nah, naaah. It's nothing crazy. It's just a few places where I be dropping bags off. The jobs are simple. Just drop off and pick up. I'm not going to tell you what be in the bags, because truthfully, I don't know every time.'

"Then he hit me with some bullshit. 'Damn. Shit. You off the street, right? I mean, you look better. Shit working out for you. Shit, you down or what?' We had come to a complete stop at the time he was telling me all this.

"I walked off. 'Nigga, I'm down. I just don't have no time for no fucked surprises.'

"He followed me like, 'Yo. How many times I got to tell you that you're good?'

"Then he gave me the rundown. 'So, Sebo is putting us together for like two weeks. My job is to make sure you know when and where to drop the bags. Now, there are only three different locations we drop bags. One is in Washington Heights, Manhattan, one is in Marcy, Brooklyn, and one is in East Harlem. I'm going to take you to all these spots and introduce you to the people you will be dropping off to. Now, all the spots are establishments. These are big-time people who own shit.'

"Then he stopped at this corner store. 'Yo. Let's go in and grab something to eat so we can sit down so I can explain all this to you.'

"So, we grabbed some food and found a table to sit at. Then he finished telling me about the drops.

'The spot in Brooklyn is in a plaza. It's a pizza joint. It's always a young girl working the cash register. You're going to know her because I'm going to introduce you to her. And if it's ever anyone besides her, don't give no one the bag, and call Sebo. Just walk back out. She'll find the perfect time for you to pass her the bag. So, pay close attention to her. This drop always takes place between nine thirty and ten every Tuesday and Thursday. Not a minute late.

'Another thing is, Sebo don't want us stopping and talking to no one. That's important. Especially at our next spot, Washington Heights, you got to be on point up there. A lot of crazy shit be happening all over that place. Once I introduce you to these people, they'll actually be looking for you. Shit, they'll see you way before you hit the spot. So, you'll have some kind of lookout for you.

'The drop-off is a corner store. They're not going to just let you walk in and then right back out. They're going make you wait a while. Shit, sometimes they won't even let you in if they think you are being followed. And if that happens, look for someone who's trying to get your attention, because they will escort you to another location. Just pay close attention. I'll introduce you to a few people who will be grabbing the bag from you. The drop is only on Wednesdays, between twelve and one.

'Now, the next stop in Harlem is pretty laid-back. So laid-back that sometimes I stop to visit my grandmother, even though I'm not supposed to. The drop is an Italian spot on 125th. Now, this dude is nice, but he's always paranoid. He will make you sit in to eat, and when the time is right, he will call you back where he prepares his food.

'In the far back of the store is a screen door that will always seem to be open, revealing a very dirty alley and half torn-down buildings, allowing you to see the next block over. His place is the only spot that sometimes you will have to bring a bag back. Drop-off time for his spot is between nine and ten.'

"Then he paused. I gave him a look like, 'Nigga, you done?'

"Responding to the way I looked at him, he said, 'Yo, you good. Is it too much?'

'I'm good. Shit, I'm ready when you are.'

Then he got all hyped up, talking about, 'Bitch, that's why I fuck with you. I knew you was real ever since that fucked-up foster home we lived in. Now, come on; let's get Pop's food to him.'

"Before you knew it, we were making drops together. I met everyone and learned my routes quick. He wasn't joking about the Heights though. That place made me feel uncomfortable. Everybody looked like they were on some sneaky shit. Other than that, everything was good. A few times when we went to Harlem, we would stop by Hector's grandmother's place. She was a nice lady. She loved Hector a lot. Sometimes she would constantly hug and kiss him. Hector asked me if I would be nice enough to stop and check on her sometimes. I told him sure."

Chapter Eighteen

And Then This

"Three years flew by. I was now sixteen. This was my new family. Strange, but they held me down like family. I mean, birthday parties, and I was a part of holiday events. That was a lot for me. I mean, I hadn't been a part of those kinds of events in a while. Shit, we even went to church every Sunday and weren't allowed to miss it. I would see the women of the family and friends at church, and they couldn't stand me. They would give me some nasty-ass looks. It was only because all the male family and friends liked me and spent most of their time around me. So, I didn't stand a chance going to the actual family events.

"But the male side of the family still made it seem like the real thing. Shit, sometimes Pop and I would do our own little thing. What really threw me off was that they wouldn't take Pop to the holiday events either. Never could figure that out.

"One night, right before I went to bed, I sat on my bed and thought about how crazy shit had played out in my life. It was like sometimes things seemed to be moving in the right direction, and then the unexpected happened. And what makes this whole thing crazy is I went to bed that night and woke up to my door being kicked in.

"Police were every-fucking-where. They had guns pointed at my head and demanded that I get on the floor. Once I got on the floor, they handcuffed me and dragged me out to the living room. Still lying on my belly, I looked around. The police were searching the house. They had on all black and were wearing ski masks. On top of that, somebody was an undercover cop, because one of the cop's voices sounded mad familiar. I just couldn't put a face to it.

"Then I looked to my left and saw Pop lying on the floor the same way I was. There was a cop kneeling beside him with his hand on Pop's back. The cop was looking up, yelling at the other cops in Spanish. Then I took a closer look at Pop, and something didn't look right. His mouth and eyes were wide open, and he wasn't moving. I whispered, 'Pop Pop?' but he didn't answer. I just broke down and started crying. Pop was dead. I just yelled, 'Please, please, somebody help him, please!'

"This one cop, disregarding everything I just said, yelled, 'Hey. She speaks English. Take her out to the paddy wagon ASAP.'

"They snatched me up and took me to the paddy wagon. When they opened the back door, I couldn't believe my eyes.

Mostly everybody that came to Pop's in the morning was in the wagon. I even saw some people that I knew from off the street. Then they put me inside.

"As soon as the door closed, I heard someone whisper, 'Yo, Ta, you better not snitch about nothing.'

"I couldn't see who said it because it was dark as shit. But I said, 'Yo, nigga, fuck you. You'll snitch before I will. I don't know shit.'

"Then it got quiet. When I got down to the station, I was really blown away. There were two big-ass caged rooms that sat opposite from each other. They had everybody I knew in them, including Sebo and Hector. Women on one side and men on the other.

"Hector yelled out, 'Yo. Tata, you good?'

"At this time, I was standing in front of an officer sitting at a desk. I looked back at him. 'Yeah, I'm good.'

"Hector, still yelling, said, 'Yo! Where is Pop?'

"I yelled back, "I think Pop is dead!'

'What you mean, you think?'

'He was just lying on the floor, unresponsive, and he looked fucking dead, yo.

"After I said that, everybody got loud and started speaking in Spanish. I think most of the yelling was pertaining to Pop, and some was just being frustrated with everything going on. The more I looked around, the more I noticed everyone I knew. Even some people from the drop-off locations.

"The cop that walked me in was now unhandcuffing me. He took me to this little side room. Inside the room were three officers, one black and two white guys. And there was another person who stood in the corner wearing a face mask. As soon as I sat down in the chair, the black officer introduced himself and his fellow officers.

'Hi, Tata. My name is Officer McGee. My two friends here are Officer Young and Officer Bowers.'

"When he said that, I looked over at the cop who was wearing the mask.

"He noticed it and said, 'Oh, him. I can't tell you his name, but I can promise you this. He knows you pretty well.'

"I was all young and didn't really have a clue what was going on. I replied, 'Oh yeah. Well. Why he hiding his face then?'

"McGee said, 'Well, honey, he can't reveal himself. He's one of us. He helped put this successful bust together. He's just here to let us know when you are lying.'

"Young said, 'Hey you. What's your real name? We know it's not no damn Tata.'

"I said, 'Why?'

"Young said, 'Because I fucking asked for it, that's why.'

"Bowers said, 'Hey. Stop being fucking smart. I'll put some of the worst charges on your ass. Fuck with me if you want. You'll go to prison right after you do juvie.'

"Not knowing the severity of this shit, my dumb ass said, 'Yo. You fucking tripping. Damn. My name is Princess Malloy.'

"Young said, 'That's all you had to say the first time.'

"McGee said, 'So, how long have you been moving drugs for the Gambino family?'

"I said, 'What drugs? And for who?'

"Bowers said, "Didn't I just say I wasn't fucking playing with you?'

"I said, 'Man, I don't know what the fuck you talking about.'

"With a smooth voice like he had no worries, the undercover cop spoke, 'The bags. The bags that you been moving. You been moving them now about three years or more.'

"I shouldn't have said shit, but I replied, 'Yeah, but I didn't know what was in them.'

"Young said, 'That's bullshit, and you know it.'

"I said, 'Look, man, they gave me a place to stay and treated me like family.'

"Bowers said, 'Yeah, in exchange for helping them move drugs.'

"I said, 'Nah. That's not true. I helped Pop out around the house and that's it.'

"The undercover cop said, 'You are a lying ass.'

"Young said, 'Who the fuck is Pop?'

"The undercover cop said, 'Some old man who was living peacefully in his apartment until Sebo took over his shit.'

"I said, 'That's not true either. That's Sebo's father.'

"They all started laughing. Then I started thinking, *If that's true, it explains why Pop could never go to any of the family functions either.*

"McGee said, 'Princess, these people who you are affiliated with are ruthless killers and drug dealers. You know that. Now come on. Help us out.'

"Before I had a chance to say another word, this tall, slender white man came in, holding a briefcase. His ass even knew my name. 'Don't say another word, Princess.'

"Then he looked at the cops. 'Hey. Do you know that she's a fucking minor? You can't question a minor without a guardian being present.'

"McGee said, 'Who the fuck are you?'

'I'm her lawyer. So, you either read her her rights and charge her or let her go.'

"The cops didn't say shit. They just all got up and left the room. The lawyer just told me to chill and not to say another word to anyone. Then this one cop came in, took me to a holding area, and handcuffed me to a bench. I sat there for hours, watching the cops call everyone one by one to the back for questioning. I knew what time it was now. They were trying to get everyone to snitch on each other.

"This shit was crazy. They had moms, daughters, sisters, and grandparents all locked up. Most of the older women and men made it home with charges, but everyone else, including females, went to jail. I watched everyone leave. I thought, *What in the fuck are they going to do with me? I'm still sitting here.*

"Another two hours passed, then some cop walked over to me and asked who I was. I told him, then he walked over to some other cops who were standing around talking. They all looked over and laughed at me. I thought, *These silly fuckers.*

"Anyway, he walked back over to me, took the cuffs off, and laughed. 'Damn, we almost forgot about you. Shit, you're free to go.'

"I thought, *Damn.* I just knew I was going to jail for some dumb shit. Like, I'm not going to front. I knew I was doing something illegal; I just didn't know what the fuck it was.

"I didn't ask no questions. I got straight the fuck up and walked out. I'm thinking they must not have had shit on me. I was excited for like five minutes, until I realized that I didn't have anywhere to go. I was like, *What am I really walking out to? Everybody's fucking locked up.* I instantly thought, *Damn, back to the streets again.*

"I hurried back to Pop's spot to grab my shit, but when I got there, the door was bolted down. I couldn't get in, and all my shit was in there. Man, this was the worst. I went down to the rental office, but no one was there. Yo, it felt like a bitch was going into a panic attack. How could my life be going so well and then, out of nowhere, end up like this? Shit, I had money in that bitch too. I had saved up a little over three racks during my time there.

"Devastated, I walked over to one of my favorite pizza shops. Along the way I saw a couple of people I knew. Some were giving me crazy-ass looks like, 'Bitch, what are you doing home?' I just looked back at them like, 'Fuck you too.'

"When I got to the pizza spot, I didn't order anything. I just found a table to sit at. Still in disbelief, I folded my arms on the table and placed my head on them. Almost in tears, I stayed like that for a while. Then, out of nowhere, I felt a tap on my shoulder. I looked up, and to my surprise, it was Hosea, this Spanish dude that used to come over to Pop's house almost every day. He was a real cool dude. I had known him since day one.

'Yo. Ta, you okay?'

'Nah, nigga. I'm fucked up right now. Didn't you hear what happened?'

'I heard. That shit is crazy, yo.'

"Then it popped into my head, *Why the fuck is this nigga not locked up with the rest of the dudes he hung out with?* I didn't say shit though. Before I had a chance to speak, he spoke again.

'What, they raided Pop's spot too?'

'Yeah, nigga. I think Pop died, and all my stuff is locked in his spot too. I'm fucked up right now for real.'

"Standing there in disbelief, almost looking like he was about to cry, he said, 'Damn. Yo. Pop. Fuck, man. This shit is a nightmare. Here, take this. I got to go.'

"He gave me some bread, then hurried out. I checked to see how much he had given me, and it was three hundred dollars. My eyes got big as fuck. He had never before hit me with that kind of money. Shit, maybe fifty or forty dollars for running to the store, but that was it.

"Now, don't get me wrong, and I'm not complaining, but that shit didn't make me feel good at all. For one, I was still fucked up, and two, I thought this nigga was a snitch.

"Man. I had put in a lot of work to get where I was, and now not only did I not have a place to stay, but I also didn't have my clothes and shit either.

"I couldn't believe it. I was back on the streets again. I mainly slept inside of the restaurants belonging to people I knew. But how long was that going to last? They were going to eventually get tired of that shit and tell me to leave. And I damn sure wasn't going back to my aunt's. That was out of the question.

"Anyway, three days passed. I finally got in touch with the superintendent of Pop's building. I told him that my clothes were in the apartment that got raided last week, and I was hoping I could get them. He was walking away from his apartment at the time and wasn't paying me any attention. So, I got a little louder, just in case his ass was deaf or something.

'Look, man, I need my stuff bad. I'm homeless at the moment. I don't have anything or anywhere to go.'

"This dude was a trip. A tall, black Dominican. Dressed in two different browns. Looked like he was wearing an old suit or something.

"Still ignoring me, he kept walking. 'I'm not taking shit out of that building. And if I wanted to, I couldn't, because the apartment is still under investigation.'

"Young, and not fully understanding what he was saying, I sort of yelled, 'Yo, all I need is my shit and I'm out. Come on, yo.'

"Then he got nasty with me. 'Hey. What the fuck did I just say? I can't let you in.'

"Yo, Mike, I'm not going to hold you. It felt like a knife cut me when he said that. I just dropped my head and walked off. And then, out of nowhere, this nigga said, 'It would be a different story if we were fucking.'

"I turned around and said, 'What?'

"He mumbled, 'You heard me. You going to give me some pussy? And don't give me that boyfriend shit, because I been watching you for the last three years, and I ain't seen you with nobody.'

"I thought, *Damn, I'm only sixteen, so that means his perverted ass started watching me when I was thirteen.* I told the pedophile ass, 'Fuck you, and if I had a dick, you could suck that too.' Then I walked out.

"Yo, I wasn't fucking that dude. I didn't give a fuck how bad I needed my shit."

Chapter Nineteen

POINTLESS

"Somehow, I managed to live in and out of the restaurants of the people I knew for a year now. Some would even lock me in them until the next morning when they opened. One of the shops I stayed at belonged to Hector's uncle.

"One day when I was wiping off the tables, his uncle walked over to me and said, 'Hey. You do a good job here, Ta, but I'm going to be closing down soon.'

"I already knew where he was going with this conversation, so I just gave him a funny look.

"He gave me this sincere look. 'Hey. I'm just not making any money here. Lately, people have just been walking right by here. I'm moving to another location. I'll give you one more week here, then you have to leave.'

"I didn't say nothing. I just kept cleaning.

"He walked off, then stopped. 'Ta, why don't you call Hector? Maybe he can help you out.'

"He had my attention then. 'Hector? Hector's in jail.'

'No. Hector is home. He been home almost a week now. Last I heard is that he was staying with his grandmother in Harlem. He said that he's supposed to be coming back here to stay with my sister next week.'

'Damn. I didn't know that.'

"He tapped my shoulder. 'As a matter of fact, come on. Let's give him a call.'

"I thought, *That's what's up. My boy's home. I know he'll make something happen.* As I was thinking, his uncle started walking toward me with the phone.

'Here. Hector's on the phone.'

"I answered, 'Yo.'

"Hector, loud as a bitch, said, 'Yooo. What the fuck? You still over there, bitch?'

'Yeah, I'm still here, nigga. I'm fucked up. I lost all my shit at Pop's. I been trying to get back ever since.'

'So, what the fuck you been doing then, yo?'

'Nigga, I been surviving. I been working in and out of restaurants just to find somewhere to lay my head.'

'Yo, Ta, I don't have no spot for you to stay, but I might be able to help you keep some money in your pocket.'

"Hey. I wasn't expecting that response, but it was better than nothing. I was like, 'Shit. It's whatever.'

"He kept talking, 'I'm over here at my grandma's now until my aunt gets a phone line in her spot, so I can do my probation there. When I get over there, I'm going to get with you.'

'Okay. That's what's up. I'll probably be here at your uncle's spot.'

"Anyway, that week came fast. I met Hector at his uncle's pizza shop. Yo, this nigga was mad different. He was just mad slick out of the mouth. He would just say anything. I always felt comfortable around him, because he never judged me, but shit, even that shit had changed.

'Yo, Ta. What the fuck? You look bad as fuck, yo.'

"That was the first thing his punk ass said.

'Yo, fuck you, nigga. I been out here in these streets. I have a reason to look crazy.'

'Nah, nah, I'm just fucking with you, but you do look mad different. You lost a lot of weight.'

'Nigga, fuck, what you talking about? What's up with getting some bread?'

"He was like, 'Peep this. Let me get my shit right, and you can start making some runs for me.'

"Yo, Mike, I'm telling you right now; the jail changed this nigga completely. I don't know what happened in there, but he wasn't the same.

"Anyway, when the time came, he had me doing small runs over to Washington, Heights. The shit was wack, because sometimes I would go over that bitch four times a day. And I know that shit was no good, because he taught me that. Then on top of that, he wouldn't pay me until the end of the day, when you were supposed to get paid for each individual run. Not to mention the little bit of money he would hit me with.

"But I was grateful, because I didn't have shit. Sometimes he would go weeks or a month without hitting me up. One time I went to a spot where he be hanging, because I was fucked up with no money. He was there, posted up with his boys. The nigga handled me almost as if I was a stranger. I guess he called his self embarrassing me with his little slick talk. He was dumb for that, because a bitch like me is built for that. You can't hurt no feelings here. Shit, I'm too cold for that.

"I laughed that shit off. I told him that I was fucked up and that I needed to hold something until the next run. He walked over to me, gave me a soft hug, and handed me forty dollars. Hector was strange, yo. He had his days where it seemed like he fucked with me and then days where he was on some bullshit. Hector was still my people. The only friend I had.

"At this time, I was completely homeless and back on the streets. Shit was rough as fuck. One day I was mad hungry. Couldn't make a dime to get something to eat. Then it came to me. I thought about the Italian shop over in Harlem. The one shop that I made drops to. The paranoid dude. Remember? He would always keep his back door open.

"I made my way over there. I even went by Hector's grandma's spot a few times, but she never answered the door. Harlem wasn't too bad. I even made a few hustles on the streets. Remember, Mike, how I said that you could see the back of the Italian dude's shop from the next street over?"

"Yeah, I remember."

"Well, one day, I crept through the broken buildings and made my way to his shop. Sure, enough the back door was open, and there was food on the table. I'm not going to front. This turned into my new go-to spot real quick. The first time I went in to grab some food, it was really hot in there. I instantly thought, *Damn, that's why he keeps the door open.* I only took small amounts of food. It was mainly lunch meat and fruit. But how long was this going to last? Not long.

"He caught me a few times. The last time, he noticed who I was. He actually cornered me in. He snapped out. Called me everything under the book. It took a while for him to notice me. I guess I could say I honestly looked fucked up. For like six months, I completely let go of myself. Real rap, I wanted to die. It felt like my life was a big joke, filled with a bunch of sorrows.

"Mike, I wasn't washing my ass or nothing. Though all the bullshit I was going through, I did manage to keep my teeth brushed. I know this might sound crazy, but that was one thing that reminded me of my father. He made up these funny games to make me always want to brush my teeth. So, those moments stuck with me the most."

Adjusting myself on the couch, I said, "Yo. You don't have to tell me, May. Shit, I know. Your ass was tripping."

"Anyway, the last time he caught me is when you came over there. I looked at your frail little ass and thought, *Nigga, you about to get your ass whipped.* That Italian dude made three of your ass."

"Yeah, right, dumbo. He would have got his ass handled. I didn't come over there for you anyway."

May started laughing. "Don't get mad, yo. Then you had the nerve to give me a hundred dollars, talking about getting back with me. Shit, I'm not going to front; I needed that money. That shit was a blessing. I also caught that number you threw at me. I wasn't going to call you, but it didn't take long for shit to get bad again, so I thought, *Shit, let me give this nigga a call to see what this job is about.*"

"Yo, May. Do you realize you just told me your whole fucking life story? Damn. Before all this shit happened, I couldn't get two fucking words out of your ass. I can't call it, but I think something else happened to you when you got shot. I never heard you talk so much. I'm not going to hold you; your life was fucking terrible."

May smacked her teeth, then fell back on the bed. "Shut up, dumb-dumb. I'm going to sleep now."

"Yeah. I bet you are. Shit, I'm sleepy too. Don't wake me up no more."

Rolling to my other side, she muffled out, "Fuck you."

Chapter Twenty

FAMILY TIES

The next morning, I was awakened by a couple of slaps to the face. "Hey. Wake up, Papi. You in here snoring all loud."

It was Auntie.

"Get up. The doctor just said that they were going to let May come home later today or early morning. Go home and clean your room. Your room is a sight. Nobody wants to come home to that."

I didn't say it, but I thought, *Shit, that's my room. Shit, she can stay in the other room.* Then I thought, *Shit, I'm definitely not cleaning that room out. There's a whole lot of shit in there.*

Standing up and stretching now, I said, "Okay, Auntie."

I got up to give her a hug. "Hey, Auntie. Where's May?"

"They took her for some tests. She should be on her way back. She's been gone a while now."

"Okay. Tell her I'll see her when she comes home. I'm about to shoot to the crib."

"Okay, Papi. Don't forget to clean the room."

It was early in the morning, and I was still tired as shit. When I got in the crib, I heard the TV on in Unc's room. I peeked in the room, but he wasn't in there. Then I heard the shower water running in the bathroom. I said to myself, *Shit, Unc must be home.* I went to my room. I was supposed to be cleaning it, but instead I fell on my bed and crashed out.

I had the strangest dream. I dreamt that I was standing alone in a park. Not one person in sight. It was daytime, but it was very cloudy. When I walked, it felt like I was drifting or floating. My surroundings seemed fake. I saw this white bench sitting a good distance from me. I started walking toward it, and the closer I got, the more I noticed that someone was sitting on it. Once I got right up on it, there was a person sitting there in a white robe or gown, their back facing me. I walked around the bench to face the person but couldn't see who it was because their head was down. I leaned closer, and I could hear this person sobbing.

I asked, "Hey, are you okay?"

I didn't get a response.

I tried again. "Hey. Why are you crying?"

What happened next blew me away like you would never believe. It was my mother, and she wasn't happy to see me.

She yelled at me, "Mike, you know why I'm crying!"

Excited as hell, I yelled, "Mom!"

"Don't mom me. You're about to do something dumb."

"Mom, I'm happy to see you. Why are you yelling at me?"

Then she started talking strange, like her words were breaking up, "That boy that shot that girl. You going to pay. Don't do it. Don't do it."

I looked away from her to gather my thoughts. Then I turned around to tell her a lie she already knew.

"Mom, I'm not..." I looked, and she was gone.

I broke down and laid on the bench. Then it got completely dark, and all I heard was, "Mike, Mike, Mike. Yo, wake up, man."

It was my uncle. He shook me out of my sleep. I jumped up, put my feet on the floor, and placed my head in my hands.

"Nephew. You all right, man?"

I just shook my head from left to right.

"Come on, neph. Get yourself together. Damn, man. You sweating all crazy and shit."

My eyes full of water, I looked at him. "Unc, I had a dream about Mom."

"I know. I heard you calling her." Still standing there with his towel wrapped around him, he said, "Yo, get up, man. Damn. What was it, a bad dream or something?"

"Yeah, Unc. She wasn't happy to see me, that's for sure."

He started walking out of the room then stopped at the door. "Well. What in the hell happened?"

I was just about to tell him, but then I thought, *Shit, he's not going to do nothing but pick up where she left off.*

"I'm good, Unc. It was just a crazy dream."

He was like, "Okay," and walked back to his room. I just started cleaning and organizing my room a little. After I had everything looking good, I went to the kitchen for something to eat. I looked in the refrigerator and noticed that Auntie had cooked my favorite—chicken, rice, and peas. I piled some on a plate, put it in the microwave, and got my eat on. While I was sitting there eating, Unc came in. He grabbed a seat, and we started talking.

"Hey, neph. What you got going on today?"

Walking to the fridge to grab something to drink, I said, "Not much. Just trying to get things in order."

"Oh okay. That's sounds good."

I already knew where this conversation was going.

"Are you still looking for work, man?"

"Yeah, I been talking to a few people about some jobs."

"That's good, Mike."

Then he got serious. "Look, Mike. No more surprises, man. I can't take that shit. I always been real with you. Never hid shit. You hurt me, man. I'm not going to lie."

"Yo, Unc. I'm sorry about that. I didn't plan on this shit playing out like this. It just did."

Honestly, I was stumbling all over my words. I didn't know what the fuck I was trying to say. All I knew was that I was in the wrong.

"Unc, I was afraid to tell you certain shit because I knew how you was going to act."

"Well, just talk, man. Shit, tell me. That way I won't be surprised."

Yo, on some real shit, I loved Unc. I told him that it wouldn't happen again and gave him a hug.

Then he said something I had never heard him say. "I know it won't because the next time I'm putting you out."

I started laughing right away, but I felt truth in what he said. Plus, he wasn't laughing along with me.

Then he changed the subject up. "I'm about to start working a new job that will allow me to be home more often. I be driving East Coast instead of international."

"Shit, that's what's up, Unc. That's great news."

Then he asked if I had seen Auntie this morning at the hospital. I told him I had.

We made some small talk. Then, after that it was time to make some moves, so I got dressed. I thought, *Shit, I need to make some bread and find out something about Hector.* I already had like an ounce of weed bagged up in nics and dimes, so I tucked that into my jeans and made my way out the door. On my way out of the building, I bumped into Auntie.

"Hey, Papi. Where you on your way?"

"Nowhere, really. Just leaving to get some fresh air."

Then she hit me with, "Fresh air. What you need fresh air for?"

Auntie was worked up. I think I had her stressing. She wasn't as happy as she normally was when she saw me.

I was like, "Auntie, why does it seem like everybody's mad at me?"

She yelled, "Papi, it's like you're doing everything wrong! I want the best for you. Do you understand that?"

"Yes, I do. I'm trying to find a job to make things better for myself."

Her voice got low. "Oh no, Mike. It's not just yourself anymore."

At this time the elevator door opened. She walked away from me and hurried inside. I know she was upset. I wasn't done talking to her, so I tried to follow her, but she pushed me away.

"Not now, Papi. I got a headache. You be careful out there."

Auntie never handled me like that. She and Unc must have had a serious talk about me. I'm not going to front. All the shit I had put her and Unc through, selling weed, the missing money, May getting shot, and now she was pregnant. I felt terrible. I thought about it, and it was too much for me. I left my building. I didn't say nothing. I just watched the elevator door close and walked out of the building. There were a few people out, chilling. I sold like half an ounce in a half an hour. It was kinda slow.

As I was walking down the block, I heard a car coming up the street, playing loud music. I didn't notice the car, but as it got closer, I noticed the niggas that were in it. It was Thug Maine and Crazy Joe. We busted it up for a few. You know, small talk.

Right when they were about to pull off, Joe was like, "Oh shit, Mike. Matter of fact, I got to talk to you." He pulled over and got out. "Come on, yo. Let's walk over here, son."

So, I followed him.

"Yo, son. I got the drop on the boy Hector."

I got hyped. "No. Real shit, yo?"

"Real shit, yo. Tonight, I can out everything that nigga got going on." He pulled me closer. "Listen, Mike. I'm fucked up right now, son. It's anything for me right now. You know I wouldn't charge you, but I need some bread bad. I got some major shit going on. You feel me?"

Almost whispering now, he said, "Listen. I can line this shit up for tonight, son. I put in some work for two of my niggas, so they owe me a favor. They not going to put in any work, but they'll be there just in case some shit gets out of hand. My boy Phunk is a beast at shaking the cops, so he's going to be the driver.

"Now, wherever Phunk goes, his boy Tinwon goes. Phunk and Tinwon are right-hand partners. There's a story out there that the way they met was they were both plotting on robbing each other. It took place in junior high school. They were both known for taking other people's shit. Then one day after school, they tried to rob each other. Shit got messy. They got into a big fight that went off and on for like two weeks.

"After they realized that they had so much in common, they squashed the beef and teamed up. They both came from broken homes, so they spent a lot of time together on the streets. The older they grew, the closer they got. These niggas have done everything from robberies and extortions to bodies. Mike, they nice, yo. I'll have everything ready for later tonight."

I don't know what it was, but the dude was quick to introduce me to some gangster shit.

"Okay, Crazy. Put it together. I'm down."

Me and Thug Maine busted it up for a second, then they left.

After that I made my way down to Willie's. Along the way I bumped into a few locals and chopped it up with them as well. I got off a few bags of weed in the process. Right when I reached Willie's door, I got a phone call from Steve.

"Yo. Mike. What up, son?"

"Not much, son. Just trying to get back."

"How you looking?"

"Still holding onto a pretty good amount of green, yo. I been over to the hospital and doing other dumb shit, but I'll be ready soon."

"No rush, son. Just checking on you."

"Yo. Steve, I got some shit I need to talk to you about when you get some time."

He got serious. "Yo. Mike, you good, right? Like do I need to come now?"

"Nah, nah, nah, it's not like that. It's about that shit that happened with May."

He was like, "Oh okay, Mike. I'll be through tomorrow morning."

"Okay, son. See you then."

I really needed to talk to Steve, because he had grown up in the Bronx, and he might know who this Hector dude was.

Anyway, after we hung up, I knocked on Willie's door.

He came to the door, eyes all big. "Hey, Mike. What's up?"

I walked past him. "What's up? Nigga, you good?"

Before I could say anything else, I smelled it. I didn't know who or where he got it from, but the kitchen smelled like crack.

"Damn, Willie. I see you found some hard."

Scratching the top of his head while walking to his bedroom, he mumbled out something. I couldn't understand what he said, but that's how he acted when he got high.

After he closed his door, I laughed and yelled out, "Oh, I know who it is now. You got it from the lady I see walking out of here from time to time."

One thing Willie hated was when somebody was in his business, but he loved being in everyone else's shit. He didn't respond because he couldn't. That coke had his ass on lock.

I just shook my head and made my way to my trap room. As soon as I got in there, I went to my safe. I didn't have much in it. Probably a little over two racks, and I really wasn't sure how much Crazy was going to charge me for putting this plot together. Anyway, I grabbed the two racks and tucked them away in my jacket.

I didn't turn on the TV. I just fell back on the couch and elaborated on a few things. I did think a few times of letting this whole thing go, but all I kept thinking was how bad this dude was and how many more people he could possibly hurt. Somebody had to put a stop to him, and I decided it would be me. But out of everything I had been through in life, somehow, I was a little naïve about the consequences behind this shit with Hector.

So, I guess after Willie's high went down, and he got himself together, he knocked on the door.

"Come on in, Willie. You good."

"Yo, Mike, I heard what you said, but I'm not going to pay that shit any mind."

Damn, I had Willie in his feelings.

"Nah, man, you know I was just fucking with you. What, you can't take a joke now?"

"Yeah, we can joke, but not about no dumb shit like that."

Laughing, I jumped up and walked to the bathroom. "Willie, you know what they say about the truth." Then I started laughing again.

He walked over to the bathroom, almost standing in the door while I was pissing. "Yeah, right. Truth hurts, my ass."

Before I had a chance to say anything else, he spoke again. "Mike, I been hearing some crazy talk, man."

Walking past him, I said, "What crazy shit?"

"That shit that's going on with May. Word is that you're supposed to be getting even with the person who shot her."

"Oh yeah. What nigga?"

"Shit, I don't know his name, but that's the shit I been hearing."

Then he went on with this story about how everything was supposed to take place. Most of the time, Willie's stories were on point, but he was off a little this time. I mean, it's true that I was about to retaliate, but somebody had fabricated a lot to him. Shit, honestly, I didn't know the plot. Only Crazy knew that. The part that concerned me was that people know about the beef between this clown and me.

"Willie, niggas are going to talk, yo. Especially the ones who don't have shit going on in their lives. The whole story you just told me was off point. Now, I am working on something, but not that clumsy-ass story you just told me."

He started laughing. "Yeah, I know how niggas do. They like to add their own version of shit to something."

Then he got really serious and close up on me. "Listen, Mike. If it was me, I would let that shit go. It's not that serious. But I can't tell you shit; you're a grown-ass man. I just want you to be careful. You like family to me. And besides, you mean the world to your aunt and uncle."

I walked away from him. "Come on, Willie, you getting soft on me, man. You always talk that gangster shit, yo."

"Yo, Mike, I'm not being soft. I just want you to be safe."

The conversation was strange. It was almost like he knew some shit was going down tonight, and he was trying to prevent it. Look, I knew Willie was good people, and he was worried about me, so I understood his concern. On some real shit. If somebody fucked with Willie, they were going to have to fuck with me too. Crackhead or not. And I knew Willie would do the same shit for me.

I was like, "Yo. I'm on point. I got it."

Anyway, we started talking about some other shit, and before you knew it, he wanted a couple dollars and some weed. We busted it up a little while longer, then Willie made his way to the kitchen. I had given him some green, so I guessed he figured he'd go roll up.

I just fell back and watched the TV screen. I didn't pay any mind to what was actually playing. After sitting there for a few, I fell into deep thought. I just thought really hard about this whole shit with Hector. And then, after pondering on it for a while, I convinced myself that this whole thing wasn't a good idea. I had to get my life in order. I was slowly losing respect and trust from Unc and Auntie. Plus, I had a seed on the way.

But Hector was still playing in the back of my mind. I didn't like the dude. I thought about the old saying, "Every dog has his day," and eventually, Hector was going to have his. Just thinking about my seed to come, I thought of my sister and decided to give her a call. I wasn't sure if she was at work or not, but I still called.

After three rings, she answered, "Hey, Mike."

"What's up, sis? What you doing?"

Besides Aunt Rebecca, all we had was each other now. The fact of me leaving home when I was younger didn't change anything. The love we had for each other was unstoppable. It seemed like the love grew stronger after losing Mom. It was just us now, so I had to make sure she was straight.

"Nothing. At work, bored."

I laughed. "Well, at least you're at work. I need a job ASAP."

"Brother, I keep telling you, there's plenty of work down here. You and your friend should come stay down here. You can come stay with me until you find a place."

"I'm thinking of doing that, sis. I just have to get a few things situated first."

"Mike, you always say that."

"No, seriously, I am."

"Okay. I can't wait. Plus, the kids could grow up together."

She was excited. I could hear it in her voice. But, man, it was going to be rough for me though. I couldn't imagine life without living in New York. I loved New York. The fast life, busy streets, cars, lights, buildings, and not to mention the rude-ass people. I know that sounds crazy, but it's real. I had grown up with this shit. It was a part of me. Moving somewhere different, with less activity, would probably put me into depression mode, but for my sister, it was worth a try.

"Yeah, cousins. They'll get to know each other really well."

"Plus, Mike, I been worried about you. I don't know why, but you been on my mind a lot lately. Mommy's already gone. Man, if I lose you, then I'll be all alone."

Damn, I thought, *If my sister had the slightest clue of what I'm thinking about doing, she'd probably drive up here and make me leave with her.* Her saying that put the icing on the cake. I definitely wasn't making that move now. I couldn't stand the thought of her being out there alone.

"Sis, relax, yo. I'm not going nowhere. I'm straight. I'll be down there before you know it."

"Like I said, Mike, I can't wait." Then she paused for a second, "Hey, Mike, I got to go. My supervisor's coming. Love you."

"Okay. Love you too."

I gave a sigh of relief now. I wasn't on the Hector revenge shit as much. I started thinking about getting this paper. And I also had it in my mind that I would strongly consider going to stay with my sister. *A change might be necessary*, I thought.

Chapter Twenty-One

PERFECT TIMING

I had my weed bagged up and ready for sale. I told Willie that I would get back with him and made my way to the block. Money was coming fast. I went back to my trap room like three times to re-up.

Everything was all love. I bumped into a few people I knew. Made some small neighborhood talk about what had been going on. Time was flying, and I got hungry, so I decided to go to my favorite spot, Manna's. I had a taste for some ox tails, rice, beans, and cabbage.

On my way to Manna's, I had to walk back past Willie's spot. Yo, real rap, I thought I walked past the lady that I had seen leaving Willie's house a few times. Yo, I had never seen what she looked like. I always saw the back of her. All I'm going to say is messy. I'll just leave it there.

I thought, *Shit. As soon as I'm done eating, I'm going to go back to Willie's and fuck with him. Since he wants to lie.*

I hit 5th Ave. As soon as I reached 125th, I heard this car horn blowing like crazy. I couldn't make out where the sound was coming from because the traffic was so heavy. I mean, on some real shit, car horns were always blowing like crazy around there, but it seemed like someone was trying to get my attention.

I said to myself, *Nigga, you tripping.*

I went inside to grab my food. I figured I'd go back to my crib and eat, so I got my shit to go. When I walked out of the door, I heard a horn blow again and again. I looked, and it was a four-door all-black BMW, doubled parked, with a female driving it. She was waving her hand at me, telling me to come over.

You know it was crazy out there, so I wasn't trying to move too fast. I crept over. I didn't have to get too close before I noticed who it was. It was Tammy. Goddamn. There was something about her freaky ass that brought a nigga instant joy. No matter how fucked up your day was, she would brighten it up.

I was like, "Yo. What's up? I never seen your ass drive anything."

"Mike, stop playing, nigga."

"No. You stop playing. I never seen you drive, yo."

She smacked her teeth. "Nigga, anyway, what you up to?"

"Shit. About to go to my crib and eat."

She was like, "Nah, nah, nigga. Get in. You about to ride with me."

I thought, *Bitch, you way too bossy.* But I ain't going to hold you. I kinda liked the shit.

"Yo. Who you talking to?"

Looking like she was trying to rape a nigga, she said, "Mike, get in. You got me sitting out here in this road like this."

I opened the door, setting my food on the floor in front of me. "Tammy, I hope your ass can drive."

She took off. "Fall back, yo. I got this."

As she was bobbing and weaving through the traffic and laying the horn on niggas, I thought, *Damn, her ass can drive.* I was just fucked up because I had known her ass for a long time and had always seen her walking.

Damn near yelling over the music, I said, "Yo! This car is nice as shit. Whose car is it?"

"It's my sister's. She's out of town. She needs me to take it to the shop."

Then she turned the music down. "And I got the crib to myself for a week."

I looked at her. "Right, though."

She turned the music back up. I had no clue where we were going. I just fell back and went for the ride. She made like five different stops, talking to all kinds of people.

I was like, "Yo. My food's getting cold."

"You good, Mike. Go ahead and eat. Just don't spill shit."

Grabbing my bag off the floor, I said, "Yo, I ain't going to spill shit. What, I look like a kid or something?"

She didn't respond. At this time, she was pulling into the mechanic's shop.

Getting out of the car, she looked back. "Hold on real quick, babe. I'll be right back."

Yo, I couldn't say shit. When she got out of the car, her ass was bulging out of her jeans. Her belt didn't do her no good. The top part of her ass was hanging over, revealing about four inches of her ass crack. My dick got hard instantly. Shit, I was hornier now than I was hungry. And not to mention the crazy-ass walk she had. *Damn* was all I could say.

She was gone for a good minute. I just sat there, ate my food, and listened to the radio. When she came back, she was enraged.

"Yo. That dumbass mechanic my sister used is a clown. He told me to have the car here by five, and he's not ready. He told me an hour."

"Damn. Who the fuck is it?"

"I don't know. Some dude named Kevinator."

"Kevinator?"

"Yeah. All I know is he better not take all fucking day."

She was worked up. I had never seen her behave like this.

Putting the trash from my food in the bag, I said, "Baby girl, chill. It's okay. That's more time we can chill together."

Then she leaned her seat back a little and turned almost completely, facing me. "Nigga, since you talking about chilling, pull your dick out. I need to get some frustration off my chest."

Words couldn't explain how much of a freak Tammy was. She was a classy freak. No whore shit. She thought like most niggas. She'd fuck you and then afterward, she was done with you until next time. She never wanted no bread from you. She had her own money. That made me think, *Why in the fuck does she fuck with me so hard? Is the dick that good? Because I know she got other niggas she be fucking on.* I guessed that would always remain a mystery because she wasn't going to tell me. She didn't get down like that, and honestly, I didn't really care.

I looked around because there were a lot of people out. Plus, she caught me off guard.

I looked at her. "Damn. Right now?"

"No, nigga, tomorrow." Then she gave me this dumb look. "Man, pull your shit out."

This shit was crazy, and I'm not going to front, a little uncomfortable too. But I pulled my shit out.

She didn't waste no time either. She licked the tip of my dick then slowly went all the way down. When she came back up, she said, "Yo, nigga, your dick tastes and smells just like weed."

I always kept my weed tucked away in my briefs. So, she was smelling that for sure. That made her really perform. She loved some green and some dick, and in this case, she was getting both at the same time.

We were parked next to a curve, damn near a traffic entrance, so I kept feeling like people were staring at us. That made my dick go limp a few times, but after a couple soft, deep strokes, I was like, *Fuck it. It's whatever. Shit, they can watch if they want.*

I slid my jeans down some more, so I could get comfortable. That way she could get the balls too. This went on for like a good ten minutes. The sound of the slurping, smacking, and now the fast, deep strokes had a nigga super gone. Shit, I thought my toes were going to curl through my boots.

Tammy was nice as fuck when it came to pleasing a nigga, or should I say pleasing herself.

She came up for air. "Yo, nigga. You watching for the mechanic?"

Lying my ass off, because I wasn't watching for shit, I said, "Yeah, I got you. You good."

She went back about her business, but this time harder. I leaned over to grab her ass.

She came up again. "Nigga, I want to sit on it."

Then she went back to sucking my dick. I was seconds away from busting when this clown-ass mechanic dude came banging on the window. Yo, I was hot, because I knew he saw what we were doing. Shit, he could have walked away and come back.

She stopped, wiped her face, looked in the mirror to fix her hair, grabbed some gum from her purse, and told me she'd be right back.

The guy that came to the car was rough-looking. He kinda put you in mind of a white Rastafarian or a beach bum. All his fronts were missing. From the way he was talking to Tammy, you could easily tell he was hood as fuck.

Anyway, I sat there for like five minutes, then they walked back to the car. She gave him the keys and told me to come on.

I was like, "Where the fuck we going?"

This whole shit was getting drawn out too much. She had me in upper Manhattan, at this tire shop in Sugar Hill. She said that they were going to be an hour fixing the car, so she wanted to walk around to a few stores to kill some time. We walked a few blocks down to a couple stores. I wasn't a store person, so I mainly stood outside until she was done. Shit, I was still horny. And watching her work her sexy ass around the way she was doing was driving me crazy.

Time flew by. Before I knew it, it was time to get back to the shop. She made one more stop at this corner, then we made our way back to the shop. As soon as we got in the car, she was like, "Yo, we about to go to my sister's crib."

I didn't say shit. I just went for the ride. And if I did say something, she wouldn't have heard me, because she turned the music up mad loud right after she said it. I didn't have a clue where we were going. All I knew was we went about ten blocks up. I thought, *What the fuck? What, we going to Washington Heights?*

We stopped on 162nd. I never really hung up this way, although I did know a few people up there. We parked and made our way to some projects. The area didn't look too bad. Anyway, we caught the elevator up to the sixteenth floor to apartment H30. Once we got inside, I noticed it had a Spanish setting. The reason I knew was because Auntie had similar things.

I asked her, "Yo, your people Spanish?"

She placed her purse on the table then threw her jacket on the couch. "Yeah, my sister is Latino. We have different fathers."

Then she started walking down the hallway. "Yo. Let me check to see if Jodie's here."

She opened the back bedroom door. “Nah, he’s not here.”

As she was walking back toward me, I asked her, “Who the fuck is Jodie?”

“Oh. That’s my brother. He stays here sometimes.”

Yo, I didn’t really have a clue of what to expect besides us fucking. I was away from my hood, in a different environment.

She walked me to the living room and handed me two remotes. “Here. Sit down. I’m going to freshen up and slide into something else.”

Then she walked off. I just sat there. Didn’t change the channel or nothing. There were a lot of pictures and strange ornaments everywhere, so I checked them out.

After not even five minutes of looking around, I heard the front door open. I thought right away, *Here we go.* A brown-skinned brother came around the corner. About five-eleven, bald head, and had his weight up.

“Yo. What the fuck you doing? Who you, nigga?”

By the way this nigga approached me, I didn’t know if I was going to get rumbling or what.

I put my grown-man voice on. “Mike. I’m here with Tammy.”

He didn’t say nothing. He walked off, yelling for Tammy.

She must have been out of the shower at that point, because I could hear her clearly.

She had to have had the bathroom door cracked, because she was loud as fuck. “Yo. What the fuck, yo? Why the fuck you yelling my name like that?”

“Who the fuck is this in my living room?”

"First of all, this ain't your fucking crib, Jodie. Second, that's my company." Almost sounding distanced, like she was putting her clothes on, she said, "Nigga, if you don't fall back..."

At this time, I was standing in my fighting stance, but I fell back a little after I heard her say, "Jodie." I thought, *Shit, this is her brother.*

They went back and forth for like two to three minutes. Then he went back to his room, grabbed something, and rushed out.

I was like, "Yo. What the fuck? That nigga mad as fuck right now."

She came around the corner wearing a tank top and some gray booty sweats. It was like I forgot about everything. On top of that, she was smelling amazing.

"Mike, ain't nobody worrying about him." Then she gave me this sexy look. "Now, come on."

She grabbed my hand and walked me into a room. It had to be her sister's, because Tammy's ass didn't live there, and this room looked like the master room. It had a leopard theme. The carpet, curtains, and blankets were all leopard. Shit, there were even small statues of leopards on the stands. I thought, *Shit. Somebody sure does love leopards.* There was this small recliner chair sitting in the middle of the room. She walked me over to it and told me to sit down. Then she stood behind me and started massaging my shoulders.

"Damn, Mike. Relax, yo. You tense as hell."

I was tense. I wasn't comfortable at all. Especially after the way her brother had rushed out. Who knew what was going through that nigga's mind? But after I took my boots, jeans, and shirt off, I felt a little at ease. Yo, her massage was something serious. Each deep caress of her fingers sinking into my shoulders had me feeling like I was drifting further and further into my chair. She did that for like ten minutes. Then she stood on the side of me.

Sliding her shorts off, she asked, "Did that relax you?"

I looked up at her. "Damn right, it did."

There was this big beanbag on the floor. She grabbed it and told me to stand up.

I was like, "What?"

"Chill, nigga. I'm going to put this in the chair, and I want you to sit on it."

I started laughing. "Girl, you a trip. You want me to sit on this beanbag?"

Sounding like she was getting frustrated, she said, "Yep. Come on, yo."

Shit, I went with the flow, but it felt weird as shit, especially after she asked me to take my briefs off. She told me to lean back and relax. I noticed that after I leaned back and got comfortable, my waist was now level with the chair arms. I thought, *Shit, I knew she was up to something.*

She grabbed my dick and started jerking it off. Then she put her mouth around the tip of it. She gave me a couple of deep, strong sucks, then came up. "Damn, nigga. I missed this dick."

Then she went back at it. I mean, she was going hard, massaging my balls at the same time. When she was done, she immediately straddled me. I thought right away, *Her ass has done this before*. She had complete control. Shit, she was using the chair to fuck me. Rocking it back and forth, she had my dick sliding in and out of her.

Whenever she was really into it, she would moan really loud but talk real low. It was always hard to understand what she was saying. All you could make out were the curse words like "Fuck, shit, and damn." I'm telling you, she was definitely one of those girls you just had to have in your life.

Grabbing her ass cheeks and watching her facial expressions was making me weak. She rode me fast, then slow for like ten minutes. Then she started coming all crazy like always. That shit always turned me on, so I started coming with her. Her ass came so hard that she fell asleep on my chest. I just sat there in thoughts of why she fucked with me so tough. She even kissed my neck a few times, and she ain't never did that before.

Anyway, I gave her ass half an hour and then woke her up. I had some shit to take care of, so she had to get me back across town.

Chapter Twenty-Two

WHY NOT

We got dressed, and she shot me back to my block. When I got out of the car, she yelled out, "Don't be a stranger! And if so, I'm going to come looking for you."

I told her, "You need to know I'm not going to hide from your freaky ass."

She started laughing and pulled off. It was getting pretty late, and more people were now moving around. The first person I noticed was Unc. He was talking to one of his friends he'd known for a long time. I mean, this dude had been around before I got there, and they were still cool. I'm not sure what his real name was, but Unc called him Big Lou. I walked over and spoke to both of them. Then I started walking down the block, but Unc asked me to hold on for a second.

After he was done talking to his old head, he told me that Auntie was still over at the hospital with May and that they should be coming home soon. He also said that he had a few things that he needed to talk to me about when he got back. I told him okay, then made my way down the block. I still had my weed on me, so I got on my grind.

Money was coming fast, and I knew really soon that I would have to re-up. So, I made my way back to Willie's before I got too low. On my way to his crib, one of my people, Shark, stopped me. He was telling me about this party that was supposed to be mad live. I wasn't the partying type, but I heard him out.

He told me that Neko was hosting it. The thing was that for a long time around Harlem, whenever Neko put a party together, it was always lit. He had come up in the hood, you know, just like the rest of us, doing his one-two. He had this thing with staying fly, even as a young boy, and he kept a nice whip. With all that going on, he made some friends that looked up to him.

Through the streets and incarceration, he had grown a street reputation. So, now he used his street credit to reunite people. That was why his parties stayed so lit.

"What you going to do, Mike?"

He must have noticed the look on my face.

"Come on, yo. You always on this fucking block."

He just kept going, "Yo. All the niggas are going. Plus, it's going to be mad bitches there."

You know, while he was talking, I started thinking that maybe this might not be a bad idea. With all this shit that'd been going on, a different environment might be good.

I responded, "Yo. Chill, nigga. Why you want me to go out so bad? Shit, I'm out here trying to get this paper."

"Nigga, 'cause you my people. And that paper, you can get that whenever."

"All right, nigga. Come grab me around ten thirty."

He was like, "Ten thirty? Nigga, you better get dressed ASAP, because it's nine thirty now."

Yo. Time had fucking flown by. I had no idea it was that late. But now that I thought about it, it had been a long day.

I was like, "All right. I'll be ready, yo."

"Okay, son. I'll be out front waiting on you."

I shot up to the crib. Nobody was home, so getting dressed fast wasn't going to be an issue.

I didn't get too crazy with the dress code. I pulled out Levi jeans, a Levi shirt, my Tim boots, and a zip-up fatigue jacket. I laid my clothes across the bed then made my way to the shower. In the midst of taking my shower, I thought, *What the fuck is taking Auntie and May so long to get home? Shit, they been over there all day.* On some real shit, I knew I should have at least been back over there to check on her.

Anyway, I got out of the shower and hurried to get dressed. Shit, the last thing I want to do was bump into Auntie and May when I was leaving. When I got downstairs, Shark was across the street, waiting on me. I'm not going to front though; I was sleepy as fuck after that shower.

I got in the car. "Yo. Where everybody at? What, they meeting us at the club?"

"I guess, yo. I mean, that's what everybody told me earlier."

Scooting my seat back to get comfortable, I said, "Right, though."

Sitting at the light now, he reached into the back seat. "Here, yo. You look tired as fuck."

He grabbed a black bag that had six bottles of Heineken inside it. Shit, I had to loosen up a little, so I grabbed one. As a matter of fact, I had three before we hit the club. That was big for me because I didn't drink like that. The beers did manage to loosen a nigga up. Shit, I had a little buzz going on now. In the process of all this, niggas from the block were calling, saying either they were there or on the way.

As soon as we walked in, we saw Neko at the entrance. We chopped it up with him for a second then made our way inside. Yo, the club was popping. Bitches everywhere. They had like four DJs and the Vibe and Ross Bros were there, so I know it's going to be mad lit. This club was a lot different from the last one I had been to. There weren't a lot of spots in here to sit. You were mostly standing up in the motherfucker. And it was hood as fuck.

We walked around, you know, getting our look on. In the midst of walking, we stopped to grab a couple beers. Finally, we bumped into a few niggas from our block. Shit, they had a nice corner spot that had a few chairs. I was feeling that, because I wasn't trying to be standing all night. Now, don't get me wrong; I was feeling nice, but I was still tired as fuck.

Everything was good. I grabbed a chair and fell back. Before you knew it, most of the niggas from the block were there except Crazy, T, and Dre. You know how these niggas acted when they saw me out. They be all crazy, because I didn't do the club shit. And with those drinks in them, they were extra with it. Shit, I was having a nice time. There were a few moments where it seemed like everything got completely quiet, and I thought about May. I had a lot going on, and I wasn't sure how I was going to handle everything.

When I came back to reality, I noticed that this girl was ogling Tom. There was a little commotion going on, then she walked off. Shortly afterward, there was a group of niggas that walked by, mean-mugging. All my niggas stood firm, like, "What?" After that, everything changed. The feeling of being cool and relaxed shifted to being intense.

You could damn near hear Tom over the music. "Man, fuck them niggas. I got something for them pussies."

He just kept on with the shit, and then niggas from the block got involved. I said to myself, *Here we go.*

Not even ten minutes later, I saw chairs and bottles being thrown. I don't know how in the hell Loc got a gun in there, because security was crazy tight, but he did. As soon as one person saw the gun, it was over. It started a chain reaction. I mean, everybody started running. They were tripping and running over people. The music cut off, and all you could hear were screams.

Tom was trying to yell over the screams. "What, bitch? What now?"

I thought right away, *This nigga's drunk and tripping.* He made his way toward the exit door, and we followed. When we got outside, you could hear voices from far away, yelling, "Fuck you, pussies! We going to get you niggas!"

Then there was yelling back and forth. It was a rap for me. I was ready to take it down. Plus, a nigga was tired.

Hump came over. "Yo. Fuck this. Let's shoot across town over to my people's spot."

Everybody was like, "Yeah, yeah, let's go. Fuck this shit," including Shark.

I told Shark straight up, "I'm done, yo. Take me the fuck home."

He was like, "All right, yo. I got you. We got to go right past your block anyway."

I'm not going to lie; I was nice as hell and feeling good. But I couldn't fuck with them. These niggas be tripping. It was crazy because people were in there actually enjoying themselves, and the club got shut down. I guess that's the reason for the saying "Black people can't have shit."

Anyway, Shark made a stop at a food joint that sold chicken and fries on the way home. He asked me if I was coming in and if I wanted anything. I told him I was good. He got out, and I stayed in the car.

The next thing I heard Shark saying was, "Nigga, wake the fuck up. You home."

I looked around and started laughing. Damn. I was sleepy as fuck. I fell asleep that fast. Me and Shark sat in the car for a sec, reminiscing about a few good times together. After the laughs, I dapped him up and made my way to the crib. Shit, it had been a long day, and I was ready to take it down.

Chapter Twenty-Three

SAY NO!!!!

As soon as I reached my steps, I heard a voice. I thought I was tripping at first, because the voice was low and sounded a little strange.

Then I heard it again. Almost like a loud whisper, "Yo."

The voice was coming from someone in the back seat of an old four-door box Chevy. I didn't have time for no bullshit, and shit seemed strange as fuck. I kept walking to my building. I grabbed my keys to open the door. Then I heard the voice again.

"Yo, nigga. It's Joe. What the fuck?"

I turned around and started walking toward the car. "What's up, nigga? What the fuck you doing?"

"What I'm doing? I been sitting here all night, waiting on your ass."

I rubbed my hands together and gave him a confused look. "Uh?"

Sounding frustrated, he slid over. "Nigga, get in."

I was fucking tired and wasn't feeling this shit at all. I got in. Somebody was smoking a cigarette, and it was dark as fuck. The cigarette smoke was making it almost impossible to see. Two people were in the front.

I couldn't really see, but you could tell he just took a drink of something.

"Mike, you tripping, yo. I put this shit together. Remember we talked about this earlier? I got a nigga that got eyes on him right now. We ready, nigga."

Yo, that shit caught me off guard like you wouldn't believe. Damn. I had made my mind up earlier, saying I would let this shit go. I wanted to say no, but everything was happening too fast. In almost a whispering voice, Joe told the driver to pull off.

Then he looked at me. "This fucking block is crazy hot, and we sitting here with all these guns on us."

I was caught up. I didn't know what the fuck to say. I wanted to tell them niggas, "I'm good. Ima let this shit go," but I didn't want to seem soft. My pride got in the way, plus the car was already en route.

I was like, "Yeah, nigga, I remember. I just didn't know that you were going to move this fast."

"What does it matter? We about to bust this nigga's ass."

Then he went on, "Yo, nigga. You know I don't play." All hyped up and shit, he yelled, "Yo, Phunk, turn that shit up."

They were listening to some Styles.

Trying to seem gangster, because I really wasn't with it, I smiled and said, "Right, though. My man."

It was the longest ride ever to the Bronx. It was like I zoned out to where I couldn't hear the music anymore. Images and voices were racing through my head like crazy. I kept hearing my sister's voice, saying, "No!! Mike, please, no!" and picturing Auntie's face screaming at me, saying, "You must be out of your fucking mind." Also, images of the crazy dream I had about my mother. It was just a mess of different thoughts. All this was taking place while Joe was drinking, Phunk was smoking his cigarette, and Tinwon was smoking his blunt. Not to mention the loud-ass music. I felt like I had no way out.

Joe reached across the seat to Tinwon. "Yo. Turn it down real quick." He got a phone call. "Yo. What's up?"

Of course, I couldn't hear what was being said on the other end, but I knew the conversation was pertaining to the hit.

Joe continued, "Oh yeah. Okay. What street again? How many people with him? Okay. Cool. I got you. Yo, don't let that nigga out of your eyesight. All right. One."

Tinwon looked back at Joe. "Yo. I'm not trying to be on no bullshit. This hit is supposed to be short and simple."

"Yo, bro, we got this."

Turning around and taking a pull off his blunt, he said, "Your boy doesn't look like he got shit. He looks scared as fuck."

Phunk found a little side street and pulled over. "Joe, talk to that nigga, man. He can't freeze up when we get there. Shit, them niggas might shoot first if they notice some funny shit. I'm not trying to be in no crazy crossfire because your boy's scared."

Joe sort of yelled, "Yo. You niggas are tripping. My people's straight, yo. He always been the quiet type. He doesn't do a lot of talking. Now, pull off before my boy loses sight of the contact." Then he looked over at me. "You good, right?"

That was my way out, but I didn't want to sound soft, so I tried to downplay it. "Yeah, I'm good, bro. I'm just tired as fuck."

At this time the music was back on, so Phunk and Tinwon couldn't hear me. I thought Joe would have asked more questions, like if I was feeling it tonight or something.

But instead, he replied, "Don't worry, bro. You'll be home before you know it. This is going to happen quick."

I just smiled at him and then turned to look out my window. It was cool outside. It wasn't really raining, but there was a nice strong mist coming down. It had to be around two thirty at the time. I was so off focus that I didn't know where we were in the Bronx. I'm not going to front; I was shook as fuck. I had never killed anybody before, but it was about to take place and take place fast.

We pulled over on this little back street. Joe got back on the phone.

"Yo. Yeah, we close to you now. Right. Yeah. We're like two blocks away, right? OK. You want us to come to you now? Bet. Be there in five."

Joe told Phunk which way to go. When we got to the lookout man, he told us where to park.

Joe reached over and punched me in the arm. "Nigga, get that shit ready. We're about to put that work in."

I didn't say anything because he got out of the car too fast. He and the lookout man stood by the back door to talk. I could hear their whole conversation because the windows were down along with the music.

I heard Joe say the lookout dude's name.

"Yo. What up, Bear?"

"What's up, nigga? You know me. I'm just trying to make some bread."

Yo, this dude's voice sounded mad familiar, and I knew a dude named Bear. He and this dude named YZ were in the music business, but when it didn't work out for them, they started hustling all kinds of shit. If you wanted it, they had it. But this was shocking. I didn't know he got down like this. I never got a good look at him. It was almost like he was intentionally hiding in front of Joe.

Anyway, I heard him tell Joe that Hector was just around the corner. He said that he was standing under a streetlight with four other people. I just sat there and listened to the whole plot. Bear told Joe that we had to be on point, because the niggas Hector ran with kept guns on them. If you hit Hector, you were going to have to hit them all because they were gonna shoot back.

Now, Hector was the only one wearing a black hoodie, and the last I saw, he was standing in the middle of the crowd, talking.

Joe must have already paid Bear, or he owed him a favor because he never asked for no bread. He told Joe to make a left at the light, and they were standing on the right, about halfway down the block.

Joe was like, "Say no more." He gave Bear a quick hug and hurried back into the car.

Yo, I ain't never been so nervous in my life. This shit was really about to go down. I mean, I'd done some shit in my life, but this shit was crazy for real. I had the gun on my lap.

Joe was like, "Let's switch seats real quick." I had to be on the passenger side. The plan was that we'd pull up, and I'd shoot.

Joe looked at me. "Get ready, nigga."

I didn't have to say shit; he saw the fear in my face. Shit, I couldn't even answer him.

Tinwon spoke. "Nigga, you better shoot. I'm serious, yo."

The light turned green and we made a left. I instantly saw the people standing to the right under the light. I also noticed that Joe pulled his gun out. He had the Mack 11 again. Before I knew it, the time was here. We pulled up. I saw Hector standing just as clear as day. Everybody standing there got quiet and looked. I pointed the gun at Hector.

Phunk yelled, "Shoot, bitch!"

I froze the fuck up. I couldn't pull the trigger. Hector and his boys all turned from the gun while reaching for theirs. I heard a door slam, followed by some shots. I looked over, and Joe was gone. Then I heard some hard, piercing sounds hitting the car. They were now shooting at us. Tinwon jumped out. He had the Glock 9 with the extended clip in it. He started shooting. All I saw were niggas falling to the ground.

Then shit really got weird. I couldn't believe this shit. A fucking cop siren rang. I thought, *Damn, they must have been watching them before we pulled up.* Tinwon and Joe both ran in the opposite direction. This was stupid, yo. Joe ran in the same direction of the niggas he was shooting at, and now niggas were running in the direction that Tinwon was running. I didn't know where all these niggas came from, but they were a lot deeper than Bear said.

However, I did notice four niggas stretched out, and one of them was definitely Hector. Phunk pulled off, cursing me the fuck out, all in the process of killing the alleys and side streets. The cops didn't stand a chance, even though the one cop car didn't follow us. Then he came to a stop.

Phunk reached back and pointed his gun at me. "Nigga. You fucking clown. I should blow your fucking brains out. Now get the fuck out of my car."

I got out. I didn't know where the fuck I was, but I did notice a train stop. I was scared as shit. The whole time I was walking, all I could hear were sirens. After stopping, hiding, and ducking from the law, I finally made it to the train. I caught the train to Harlem. The whole ride, I kept bouncing back and forth between sleepiness and what just happened.

As soon as I reached my building, I gave a little sigh of relief and prayed that this was all a nightmare. When I got inside my apartment, it was quiet and dark. The only light on was the bathroom. Yo, I was mentally fucked up, but the severe sleepiness overwhelmed the drastic thoughts I had running through my head.

I opened my bedroom door, and May was lying on my bed, asleep. Well, at least I thought she was. There were bags all over the floor, making it difficult to get around. I just grabbed a blanket from my closet and lay on the floor.

After not even two minutes of lying there, May whispered, "Mike, you good?"

I whispered back, "Yeah, I'm good."

I think May sort of expected something. For one, she knew I usually didn't come in this late. It had to be at least 4:00 a.m. She was the one who worked the night shift, not me.

She whispered again, "You sure?"

I didn't respond. I just closed my eyes and fell out.

Chapter Twenty-Four

THE NEXT DAY

"Papi, wake up. Why you lying around like this? It's ten o'clock."

Auntie was used to me being up. I was an early bird from day one, so she was on me.

I responded, "Auntie, I'm tired. I hung out for a while last night."

"Well, at least get up on the bed. You in the way. I'm trying to help May get her stuff situated."

I thought May needed a little help getting around. Maybe a hand with her shower and other things.

Anyway, Auntie told me that May was in the living room, watching TV. I got up on my bed and fell back out. When I woke up, I looked at my clock and it was two something. I thought, *Damn, I slept my ass off.* Then reality kicked in. I instantly thought about last night. I rolled over to get out of the bed, and I noticed May sitting on the corner of the bed with her back facing me.

I was like, "Yo, May, you all right?"

Sobbing and wiping her eyes, she cried softly, "Mike, please, please tell me that you didn't have anything to do with the shooting last night in the Bronx."

I rolled over in a sitting position on my bed. "What? What are you talking about, yo? I—"

I didn't get a chance to finish. "You know they got Joe. It's been on the news all morning. Now they're looking for two other suspects."

I thought, *Two? There were four of us.*

She walked over to sit by me. "Mike. Why? You didn't have to."

She kept on, "Damn, yo. I told you, I fuck up everyone's life I come in contact with. This shit is fucking crazy. I'm fucking pregnant. Never thought in a million years that that would happen."

The crying had stopped, and now she was serious. "I feel you. That nigga ain't shit, but he wasn't worth you, yo. This is the closest I've felt to a normal life since my father died."

I leaned all the way back on my bed.

"And your aunt. All she talks about is what a good person you are and how I'm so lucky to have you as a baby father. When you tell her—"

I stood up. "Yo, ain't nobody telling her shit. You hear me? I swear." I started pacing the floor. "Look, I got like eight racks put up. It's mainly Steve's, but he'll understand. We're going to my sister's spot in Georgia."

"When?"

"We're leaving today."

"But I have a few important appointments coming up this week."

"Well, I'm going to have to send for you later, because I got to go."

She cut me off. "Nah, nigga. What the fuck? I'm leaving too."

I was pacing the floor bad. Then I reached for my phone to call my sister. When I looked at my phone, I noticed like ten missed calls from Steve. I thought, *Steve? What's up with this*? Right in my thought process, the phone vibrated again. It was Steve.

I answered, "What's up, son?"

This nigga sounded distraught. "Yo, son. Shit's fucked up right now, yo."

I was like, "Calm down, yo. What's wrong, yo?"

"Yo, two of my cousins were gunned down last night in the Bronx, yo."

Yo. It was like my heart stopped. I ain't never felt a pain pierce my soul like that. This shit had done gotten ten times worse.

I played it off and yelled, "What?"

"Yeah, real shit. And they locked the boy, Crazy, up. Look, Mike, I know he be over there real heavy on your block." Then he hit me with the question. "Yo, Mike. You know anything about this?"

I'd never heard this nigga talk like this. It was almost like he was ready to go to war with me.

One thing I never did was lie to Steve about anything. We were way too close for that and always kept shit real with each other. But this shit was way too deep. How in the fuck was I supposed to explain this shit to him?

"Yo, that's crazy as fuck. I haven't heard shit. I been in the crib most of the day."

"Mike, you're my man, but something has to be done about this. And it's crazy because I know it's going to involve some of your people. I'm sorry, bro, but it is what it is. Lie low."

Then he hung up.

Yo, I'm not going to front. I broke down. My childhood friend, my ace, my right hand, my go-to man would most likely be no more after this. If Steve found out that I had something to do with this, I was done. He probably wouldn't want to, but he'd have someone murk me. For one, I lied to him, saying that I didn't know shit about it. I mean, I could have at least told him that I needed to talk to him and try to explain that what happened wasn't intentional. But knowing Steve, shit was still going to go down some way.

Shit, with all this stuff going on, it made me more eager to see my sister. I should have waited a few before I called her though. I had way too much shit running through my head, but I was anxious and ready to leave. I looked over at May, and she looked worried. She got up, looked back at me, and turned the TV on.

I just put my head down and started dialing my sister.

She picked up on the third ring. "Hey, Mike."

"Hey, sis. What you doing?"

"Well, I'm at work right now. Why? What's up?"

"Oh, my bad. Sorry about that, sis."

"No, you okay. If I hang up, it's because my supervisor walked in."

I tried to downplay what I said next. "Okay. I didn't really want much. Just letting you know I'm coming down."

She got very excited. "What do you mean, not too much? That's great. When you coming?"

"Well, I'll probably leave today."

"Today!!! Mike, stop playing. Are you serious?"

"Yes, sis, I'm dead serious."

"But Mike, I just spoke to you, and you never mentioned that you would be coming this soon."

I shouldn't have said what I said next, but I wasn't thinking clearly. It only sparked suspicion.

"I know, sis, but something came up."

May threw the remote next to my leg to get my attention. She pointed at the TV. When I looked up, there was a picture of Joe in the right corner of the TV screen. There was a news reporter standing in front of the location where everything took place.

The news reporter said, "Police are still searching for two very armed and dangerous suspects who played a role in the brutal murder that took place in the Bronx."

My sister must have been talking to me, and I didn't hear her. The news had me distracted.

She yelled, "Mike. Do you hear me?"

I lied and said I did, but I really didn't.

She continued, "Mike. What's going on?"

"Sis, I'll tell you everything once I get down there."

She interrupted, "Mike, I'm calling Aunt Wilma now."

I yelled, then I spoke really low. "No, sis. Please don't."

"Why?"

"Because she's not going to want me to leave."

Her voice sounded like she was about to cry. "Mike, I gotta go. My supervisor is coming."

"Well, look, I'm going to—" She hung up. All I heard was the dial tone.

She knew something was wrong. She'd never heard me talk like that, but I couldn't explain it to her. This was way too much, and I knew she wasn't built for it. On top of that, we were all we had. I felt terrible.

Anyway, even after I asked her not to call Auntie, guess what she did? She called Auntie.

The morning got really crazy. Slowly but surely, everyone got involved.

Auntie came busting into the room. "Hey, Papi. What's wrong with you?"

Still sitting on the bed, I looked up at her. "Auntie. What you talking about?"

"Why in the hell did Tiffany just call me crying, talking about you coming down there today?"

"Yeah, I'm trying to put something together."

She cut me off. She stood right in front of me and grabbed my face by the mouth like you would do a little kid. The look on her face was serious.

While still holding my face, she bent over and got really close to me and spoke softly but harshly, "Papi, I know when you're fucking lying, so stop fucking lying to me."

Every time I would try to put my face down, she would yank it back up.

She got loud. "Papi, tell me!"

Auntie knew that this had to be something serious, and I could tell that she was getting scared. It was like she was seeing a different person. She wasn't used to me acting like this.

She balled her fist up. "Papi, I'm about to fuck you up."

Right when she was about to hit me, May spoke up. "Mike, tell her."

She quickly focused her attention on May. "Oh, you know?" Then she walked over to May. "Tell me, May."

I didn't notice it, but at this time the shit was right back on TV again.

May looked at Auntie and then pointed at the TV screen.

She looked at May. "What? This?"

May shook her head in a "yeah" like motion.

Auntie kinda laughed, but it wasn't in a good way. "You fucking serious? This shit we been seeing on TV all morning?"

May didn't say anything.

Auntie went from laughing to crying. She looked at me and sat on the bed. I knew Auntie, and I knew she didn't play no games, so I knew something was about to happen.

So, I was thinking this would be a good time to go to the bathroom. I stood up. I probably got about four steps. Auntie jumped up and started cussing me out in English and Spanish. Then she punched me like forty times, it seemed like. Exhausted now, she fell to the floor, still crying. I felt so bad. I honestly didn't know what to do. Unc was in his room, asleep. I guess all the commotion woke him up.

He came racing down the hallway. "What the fuck is going on in here?"

Since me and Unc had had some real-live talks and he was a male figure, I felt a lot more comfortable talking to him, even though I knew he wasn't trying to hear this shit.

I said, "Unc, I'll tell you."

I wanted to talk to him in private. Wasn't nothing soft about Unc. He'd get in your shit with a quickness. But he had done some gangster shit in the past, so I'd figured he would understand me. I walked off, hoping he would follow, but instead he wanted to know why his wife was crying and on the floor, so he walked right by me.

He yelled at her, "What the fuck is wrong with you?"

She jumped up. "Ask his dumb ass."

She started walking toward him and squeezed around him to leave the room and said, "Tell him, Papi. Tell him you done killed some people."

Unc looked at me. "What's she talking about?"

I looked at May. "Yo, leave the room real quick. Let me talk to my uncle."

She got up and walked out.

Unc closed the door. "So what's going on?"

Walking back to sit on the bed, I said, "Unc, I didn't kill nobody, but I was in the car with the people who did the shooting."

He grabbed his head and started scratching his forehead. "How in the hell did you put yourself in that kind of predicament?"

"I was trying to get back at this dude for shooting May, so I talked to Joe about it. He put the shit together so damn fast it was crazy. I really wasn't with it, Unc. It was more talk than anything. I tried to back out, but I didn't want to look soft after I was the one who initiated the whole thing."

"Damn, nephew. I don't really know what to say. You fucked up bad though. What the fuck happened?"

"Unc, the shit that's been on the news all morning."

He got loud. "You talking about the shooting in the Bronx?"

Looking like I knew I fucked up, I shook my head and said, "Yeah."

"Man, they said three fucking people were killed. I saw it earlier on the news."

Damn near in tears because reality was sinking in by the second, I said, "I fucked up, Unc. I don't know what to do."

Unc was hurt. I saw it in his eyes. He'd been taking care of me all this time since I was a child. And I'd failed him in the worst way. Since he loved me like a son and was always there for me, his natural fatherhood response kicked in.

"We got to get you out of here. They going to come looking for you. You might not think they know, but they're working on some shit right now."

Then he walked over to me. "Come on, get the fuck up. Ain't no use looking crazy now. What you going to do?"

I stood up and grabbed my phone. "Well, I called Tiffany and told her I was coming down there."

"What she say?"

"She said okay."

"Well, get your shit together. I'm going to grab my truck and bring it to the block so you can bring your stuff down."

"Okay. I just got to go to Willie's to grab my money and green."

Unc was on his way out the door when he looked back. "Green? What you going to do with that? You can't take it with you."

"I don't know. I got to find somebody who can hold it for me. I think Willie knows my code. With me being gone for a while, he might try something crazy."

He gave me a funny look and said, "Just bring the shit here. I'll put it somewhere."

Unc was mad as fuck with me. And now he had to deal with Auntie being upset.

After Unc walked off, I went to the bathroom to get myself together. On my way out, I noticed May sitting in the living room.

I walked over and sat beside her. "Yo. You good?"

"Nigga, do I look good?"

"Yo. I'm just asking."

"Well, don't ask no dumbass shit like that. No, I'm not good. I'm fucked up, yo."

"Listen. I want you to stay here until I get shit together for us down there."

"Mike, I'm telling you right now, if you leave me here, I'm out. I'm going to find a way to get rid of this baby, and I'm going back to the streets. Point blank."

"Yeah, that's real fucking smart. Look, I don't have time to argue with you, May. I got way too much going on right now."

I walked away from her and went back into my room to pack before Unc got back with the truck. I stuffed most of my things in my book bag and an old big army bag that Unc had. I was rushing like crazy, so I really wasn't paying attention to how I was packing. Whatever I saw, I just packed it. I knew how Unc was. Whenever he was trying to do something or go somewhere, there was no waiting around. He was out. I had to get moving. I still hadn't made it to Willie's.

I set everything by my bedroom door and made it down the hallway. Auntie's door was open a crack. I knocked lightly, which made the door open a little more. I felt bad and wanted to say something to her, but I didn't. She was balled up, lying on the bed, rocking back and forth. I just looked at her then closed the door softly.

While I was packing, I gave a thought to May coming with me, and I came up with, *It shouldn't be a problem. I mean, if she needs to see a doctor, she can see one down there.*

So, I walked to the living room door entrance and was about to tell her, but she was gone. I searched the house, and she was nowhere to be found. I just dropped my head. Her dumb ass had done gone walking or maybe just left for good. Shit was just getting worse by the second.

I ran downstairs looking for her. I looked up and down the block but didn't see her. I tried to ease my mind by thinking she just went for a walk and would be right back.

On my way to Willie's, niggas were looking at me mad funny. I didn't say shit. I just kept moving.

Chapter Twenty-Five

RUNNING

I knocked on Willie's door. It took a minute for him to open it. I thought, *I know he's here; his ass never goes anywhere.* This shit was stupid. The dude tried to have a conversation with me with the chain holding the door closed.

"Yo, Mike. What's up?"

I snapped, "What? What you mean, what's up? Open the fucking door, yo."

As soon as I heard the chain come off the latch, I pushed the door open. "Yo. What's that about? You talking to me from the door now. What, I'm the Eagle?"

He looked back for some reason, and I noticed his bedroom door closing slowly. Then I thought, *He's got that one girl over here. The one that I always see walking away.*

I was like, "Man, all you had to say is that you have company."

Following me to my trap room, he said, "It's not that, Mike. It's you. You fucking up bad. I told you that May was going to get you fucked up. You know news finds me, and I heard about Crazy. And one of the niggas that got killed was the nigga that shot May."

"Willie, I just came to get my shit and I'm out."

While I was emptying my safe out, he said, "Look, Mike, I love you like a son, but we can't do this anymore. I don't want you coming back down here. You're hot as fuck. The cops are going to be back and forth from here and your crib like crazy, because everyone knows you be down here. The only reason why I ever fucked with you in the first place was because you were laid-back. Now I don't know who the fuck you are."

I stuffed my money in my pockets and my green in a brown shoe bag and looked at Willie. "Yo. You seriously acting weak like that? Nigga, fuck you. You're supposed to have my back, nigga. Get outta my way."

I made my way out the door and slammed it behind me. On some real shit, though, Willie's point of view was valid. I was acting weak for no reason. He never had that kind of heat focused on him, and now the cops would be harassing him. *Damn,* I thought. *My boy's mad at me too. Everything's going downhill on me.*

I made my way down the block. I noticed Unc's truck parked out front. He wasn't inside, so I caught the elevator up. As soon as the door opened, I saw Unc standing there with my bags. He told me to take the bags downstairs and to give him the weed so he could put it away. He said Auntie was up, and he didn't want me getting her worked up again.

I told him okay and caught the elevator back down. I stood on the bottom floor and waited on Unc. I didn't want to be standing outside with bags. Niggas were already looking, so I didn't want to give them something else to talk about. It didn't take long for Unc to come down. We shot to the truck. I did notice a few people looking, so you already knew how far that was going to go.

Anyway, we pulled off. Unc said he was taking me downtown to Grand Central Station to catch an Amtrak train to Georgia. Unc was mad as fuck at me, but he was also worried about me too. He kept asking what I was going to do now and how long I planned on running. I told him I really didn't know.

For about four blocks, the ride got quiet. Then he asked, "You got enough money?"

Reaching for my book bag in the back seat, I said, "Yeah, Unc. I'm good on bread."

Rubbing his forehead while switching through traffic, he said, "Nephew, I really don't think you realize how much shit you done got yourself into. All your mother asked me to do was to take care of you, and I failed her. Do you even know why she sent you up here to me?"

Yo, it touched me deep when he said that. My eyes got slightly watery. "Nah, Unc. I think I know, but I'm not sure."

"Because we did such a good job with our boys. That's why. She was hoping the same for you. Look, I know I wasn't the best coming up. I done some wild shit, and I did a lot of jail time from the results of it. Sometimes life can throw you curveballs, but I thought with the way we raised you that you wouldn't have to go through the type of shit I did. But what happened is done, so now you got to make the best of it."

"I know, Unc. I fucked up bad. I'm sorry I let you down. I'm just going to try to let this shit blow over and see what happens."

"Nephew, whoever you were with, those dudes are going to put you there. Believe me, they're not taking no murder rap for you. I'm telling you straight up. When they catch up with you, you're going to do some time. Even if you weren't the shooter, the conspiracy of being there is serious. You can only run so long, nephew, and usually when they catch up with you, it's the worst time."

I just shook my head. The rest of the ride was pretty quiet besides the music that played in the background. After we found somewhere to park, we went inside to grab the ticket. Everything just seemed so strange. I couldn't believe that this was happening. The train I was catching was like forty minutes out, so we found somewhere to grab a bite to eat. Before I knew it, it was time to leave.

Unc helped me with my stuff up until we reached the top of the terminal. He gave me a big hug, told me to take care, and said he loved me. I told him the same. This was the first time in my life seeing Unc cry. He just didn't stand there and cry, but when he turned to walk away, I noticed tears rolling down his cheeks. This had to be devastating to him. He'd practically raised me from a little kid. I was like a son to him. I couldn't even say nothing to him because at the time I was crying, and I didn't want him to hear it in my voice.

I just turned away and caught the stairs down to the train. When I reached the bottom floor, where the train was, I noticed that there were only a few people waiting on it. I thought, *Damn, this is strange as fuck.* I mean, I'd never caught this type of train anywhere, but from watching TV, the station always looked packed. It was like I could just choose anywhere to sit, so I found a good spot in the back. As soon as I sat down and got comfortable, crazy thoughts of everything and everybody I ever knew started running through my head. It was too much, yo.

Anyway, some time passed, and this lady started collecting the boarding passes from the few people who were on my section of the train. When she reached me, I looked at her. She looked mad familiar. I thought, *I know this lady from somewhere.* I just couldn't remember. Shit just got really fucking weird. The people who were riding in the same cab with me were talking loud, and their voices sounded familiar as well. I thought, *I'm fucking tripping, yo.*

The next thing you know, the lights went completely out. I started yelling, "Yo, yo! What the fuck?" Then the lights started going off and on really fast, like some disco shit. In the process of the lights going off and on, I caught a glimpse of the lady who took the boarding passes. She was yelling, "Everyone brace yourself! The front part of the train has come off the track!"

My heart dropped instantly. *This can't be fucking happening.* I grabbed the metal rail in front of me to brace myself and started praying. Then there was a big bang, and it got completely dark. Right after that, I felt somebody pushing and pulling me.

I was like, "Yo, get the fuck off me."

It was like every time I got pulled or pushed, I could see a little light. I was trying to fight back, but I couldn't. This shit was crazy

Then I heard a voice, "Nigga, get the fuck up. Get up, yo."

Then the pushes turned into punches. "Yo, get the fuck outta my car, yo. You home. You over there making all those fucked-up noises. What the fuck is wrong with you?"

I looked, and it was Shark. I thought, *What the fuck. Was I fucking dreaming?*

I looked at him and said, "Nigga, I thought you already dropped me off."

He gave me this disgusted look, like he was aggravated. "Nigga, I didn't drop you off. I took your ass to the next party with me and left your ass asleep in the car. Now get outta my shit, yo. I'm trying to go home."

The End

CPSIA information can be obtained
at www.ICGtesting.com
Printed in the USA
LVHW051919280122
709476LV00011B/1458

9 781662 912979